Alter, Judith
    Luke and the Van Zandt County War.

0

Luke
and the Van Zandt County War

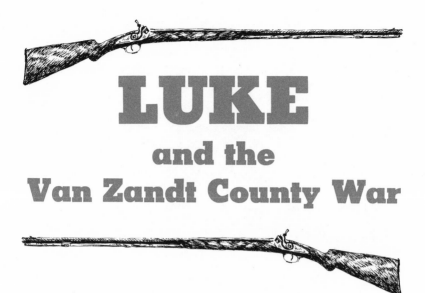

LUKE
and the
Van Zandt County War

A NOVEL
by
Judith MacBain Alter

illustrated by
Walle Conoly

A SUNDANCE BOOK

TEXAS CHRISTIAN UNIVERSITY PRESS • FORT WORTH

Alt

Library of Congress Cataloging in Publication Data

Alter, Judith MacBain, 1938–
   Luke and the Van Zandt County war.

   Summary: A fourteen-year-old girl relates how Van Zandt
County withdrew from Texas after the Civil War.
   [1. Van Zandt County (Tex.)—History—Fiction.
2. Texas—History—Fiction]   I. Title.
PZ7.A46358Lu   1984   [Fic]   84-101
ISBN 0-912646-88-8

Designed by Whitehead & Whitehead
Illustrations by Walle Conoly

For my mother

I

WE ALMOST LOST LUKE in the Van Zandt County
War and by then I'd come to care for that undersized,
skinny, know-it-all kid. But nobody could have told me, that
spring night in 1867, that I'd ever learn to tolerate him, let
alone care about him. It was pure dislike the first time I saw
Luke Widman.

I'd gone out that evening to watch a grand spring storm,
the kind that turns the sky black and bends the trees near to
the ground. Lightning burst across the sky, outlining the next
house down the road towards town, and thunder pealed so
loud I jumped in spite of myself. I was thoroughly enjoying it
when Pa called.

"Theo? You best come in out of that storm."

"It's all right, Pa. Lightning's not gonna get me."

"Maybe not," he told me in that dry tone of his, "but a chill
might. Young girls shouldn't be out in the rain."

But he didn't insist. Pa usually didn't make me do much of
anything unless it was real important, and I'd learned to sense
out those times. This wasn't one of them, so I stood there and
breathed deep, smelling the wet pines and the funny musty
smell that comes from the ground in a good, heavy rain.

Pa was reading in the office-study that formed half of our house. Really, it was a cabin that was like two separate houses, connected by a porch that ran between them. On one side of the porch was Pa's room; the other one-room portion served as kitchen and parlor and my bedroom besides. The rooms were log and each part seemed isolated. What held it together as one house was a huge roof that covered both rooms and the porch, or dogtrot as it was called, in between.

I didn't like the idea of living in a house called a dogtrot cabin, and that porch would be drafty and cold when winter came, I knew. But this cabin was the doctor's and one reason Pa decided to stay in Canton less than a month earlier. He could practice medicine in the same cabin the previous doctor had used. So here I was, living in a cabin made of sawed timbers and chinked with clay, with a crooked brick fireplace that someone had built with homemade bricks and more speed than care, I suspected.

The house was purely impossible to clean, not that I cared much about cleaning house anyway. But every time I'd sweep, dirt flew back in through cracks in the walls and welled up through holes in the board floor. It even sifted down from the roof, through the open rafters. I'd put some chintz curtains, carefully packed in Mississippi, in the three lone windows, one on each outside wall, but they didn't help to brighten the place much, and lots of times I just dreaded going in there.

This particular night, I stood as near the edge of the roof as I could without getting wet and watched the rain turn the red dirt road into a crazy pattern of little puddles and rivers. There was no denying that I felt sorry for myself—fourteen years old, my mother dead less than two months, my father lost in his grief, and me having to keep house when I had no idea which was the business end of a broom.

Those were the black thoughts going through my mind when a flash of lightning silhouetted a figure coming down the road. I had only a brief chance to look, but it was long enough for me to see a bedraggled boy, younger and smaller than me, picking his way through the puddles barefoot, with his shoes in his hand. I hoped he was going somewhere, anywhere else but to our cabin, but there was precious little

2

chance for that. Our cabin was on the far edge of town, with the next house a good three miles down the road.

He marched right up on the dogtrot with me, shook his head so that water flew in all directions, and smiled like it was a sunny day and he was perfectly dry. I decided he didn't have a brain in his head.

"Evening," he said. "It's a fine storm, isn't it?"

"I guess." I wasn't going to be cordial to someone who apparently didn't have the sense to stay out of the rain.

He appeared not to notice my cool welcome. "I need to see the doctor," he said, still smiling.

"Sorry. He's retired for the night. Come back in the morning."

"Oh, I'll just wait here, if you don't mind." He nodded vaguely at the floor, and I realized with amazement that he intended to camp there until Pa woke up. I opened my mouth to reply in no uncertain terms that I did indeed mind, when Pa called out the door and made a liar out of me.

"Theo, do I hear you talking to someone?"

The boy's eyes widened and he stared at me, barely whispering "Theo?" in a tone of disbelief. Now, I was always proud of my name, being named as I was after my grandfather and father, both of whom were Dr. Theodore Burford, but still I was a little sensitive about having a boy's name. I didn't mind as long as nobody made a fuss, but I wasn't pleased to have this young kid looking like he'd uncovered one of the seven great wonders of the world.

"It's nothing, Pa. A patient who can come back in the morning."

"I ain't a patient!" he yelped indignantly.

I gave him a frozen look which I thought would silence him, but he went on. "I came to talk to the doctor."

By this time, Pa had come to the door of his study and stood looking at both of us. He was a tall man, thin and stooped since he'd come back from The War, and now he stood holding one hip as though the place where a bullet had hit him ached. Probably, in that rain, it really did ache, but Pa never complained. Even now, he had a smile for me and a welcome for Luke. He stood there and rubbed one thin hand

3

through his curly salt and pepper hair, and then asked me, "Theo, child, where are your manners? Invite this young man in out of the rain."

"Sorry," I muttered, leading the way into Pa's study.

The boy followed me, shoes still in hand, and stood in the middle of the cabin floor, oblivious of the wet puddle he was slowly dripping into the only rug we owned, a faded old hand-braided one of considerable size. He stared spellbound at Pa's office, with its two glass-front bookshelves, crammed full of thick, well-worn medical books, and its shelves of glass jars and bottles with digitalis and tincture of iodine, a gargle of chlorate of potassium, calomel to stimulate the secretions and salts to stimulate the bowel. On one wall hung a huge anatomical chart showing the body's bones and organs. In front of it sat Pa's roll-top desk, a battered, worn one that the last doctor had used. It was nowhere near as fine as the gleaming polished desk Pa had before. I'd complained about it just once, and he told me, gently like always, that we were very fortunate to find a doctor's office with equipment and medicines, since he hadn't brought any of his from Mississippi.

Anyway, that boy just stood there staring, and Pa let him take his time. He adjusted his spectacles, closed the book in his hand and carefully marked the place, and finally cleared his throat to get the boy's attention.

Luke knew he'd been called on. He whirled around and without any how-do-you-do or anything said, "I came to learn to be a doctor."

I nearly laughed, but Pa didn't seem to think it was funny at all. He just said, "I see," in a calm tone that made you think he was considering the matter. Then he went on, "You want to learn to be a doctor. Commendable. Very commendable."

The word puzzled the boy, I could tell, but he went bravely on. "My pa says I could appre . . . pren . . ."

"Apprentice," Pa supplied gently.

"Yessir, apprentice myself to a doctor and that's how you learn." This time he said the word slowly and carefully, marking it in his mind.

I was bursting to suggest sarcastically that he was a little young, but Pa seemed to be taking all this so seriously.

"Well, apprenticeship is certainly one way to learn . . . forgive me, I don't think I know your name."

He hung his head just a moment, realizing his social error. "I'm Luke Widman."

"Pleased to know you, Luke. I'm Dr. Burford, and this is my daughter, Theo."

Luke nodded in my direction and mumbled, "We met outside," then riveted his eyes on Pa.

"Luke, how old are you?"

"Near fourteen."

Full of disbelief, I stared again at him, sure that he was a year or two younger than me and just didn't want to tell Pa. But in the dim light thrown by the kerosene lamp I saw him more clearly than I had outside and knew that he was small for his age and thin, with the look of a boy who had never eaten well, not from poor appetite but from lack of good, nourishing food. I stood a good inch taller than him, and though thin myself, I made him look like a skinny rail.

Pa, meanwhile, was considering things in his own deliberate, sometimes painfully slow way. "Fourteen, you say? It's a mite young to do much doctoring. Why did you come tonight?"

"Pa left today," he said matter-of-factly, "and he said best thing for me to do while he was gone was to learn a trade. He said I should come to you."

"Oh. Kind of him. Where did he go?"

I guess Pa was thinking maybe Luke's father had gone to Tyler or someplace and would be back in a day or two, because Pa's eyes really opened wide when Luke said, "West. Don't know where exactly. Pa just had to get going." For the first time, Luke looked a little uncertain, even scared, and I almost felt sorry for him.

"He left you behind? What about your mother?"

"She died," he said flatly. "'Bout a year ago. Pa ain't been the same since, and he couldn't stay here no more." Then he added defensively, "But I can take care of myself."

"Oh, I'm sure you can," Pa assured him, while I listened with a sinking heart. I knew we were going to end up saddled with this boy, as though we didn't have enough troubles of our own.

"You want to stay with us, is that it, Luke?"

"Yessir," he said anxiously. "I'll work for my keep. I work real hard, took care of our whole place this past year."

7

"Place?" Even my pa, the most patient, understanding man I knew, was having trouble digesting all this. "You have a place?"

"We have a little patch the other side of town, raise some cotton and vegetables. Pa just shut the door when he left this evening, said it'd all be there when he came back. I'm to kind of keep an eye on the place . . ." His voice trailed off as he stared, waiting for a verdict. Pa was silent so long that Luke rushed on with another defensive statement. "I can always go back there . . . I mean, if you don't have room . . ."

He paused because Pa and I both stared silently. It was like we were hearing an echo of our own lives. His mother dead, his pa just walking away from the house he'd called home. I felt a twinge of nastiness that I didn't have more sympathy for this boy. He was in the same place I was, only worse. At least I still had Pa. But I couldn't feel sorry for Luke. I was feeling too sorry for myself. There just wasn't room for him in that cabin or in my heart.

Finally, Pa brought his mind back to Luke's question. "No, no, son, that's not it at all. It's just hard for me to hear your story. Of course we have room."

Of course we do, I thought, but where? Pa'd have to figure that one out, since he was the one doing the inviting.

Luke was full of gratitude. "I thought maybe I could keep the vegetable garden going out to the farm and bring you some stuff."

Pa smiled for once. "That would be a help, wouldn't it, Theo?"

I merely nodded, not liking the turn things were taking at all.

It was settled before I knew it. Luke was to sleep on a pallet on the floor in Pa's study, and I had to fix the pallet! My mood echoing the still-blowing storm outside, I marched across the dogtrot to get blankets, nearly slamming the door on the way and prevented only by the sure knowledge that it would disappoint Pa if I let my anger show.

I guess Luke took Pa's mind off his grief, because when I came back into the study, they were having a cheerful visit.

"It'll be nice to have another man around the house, Luke,"

he said, which hurt my feelings something fierce. I bit my lip hard as I folded blankets on the floor to make Luke a pallet. It struck me that they would share more with each other than with me; sleeping in the same room, they'd share confidences just like Mama and I used to do when Pa got called out late at night. And I feared Pa would start to take Luke on house calls, instead of me, and turn to him for comfort and companionship. Jealousy ran through me like a green fire.

Without a word to either of them, I left suddenly, slamming the door behind me this time and not caring if Pa was disappointed. I threw myself on the makeshift bed—an affair of poles and slats covered with a pad—and lay still listening to the rain, now a gentle patter on the roof since the worst of the storm had passed.

Why, I wondered, had this happened to me? Why couldn't we be back home in Mississippi, with everything the way it used to be before . . . before The War, before Mama died.

I could barely remember back that far. Life was very different before The War changed everything. Especially, it changed Pa from the happy, always-laughing man I could now barely remember. I was eight years old when they fired on Fort Sumter. Even for a year or so after that, my life was really nice. We lived in Green City, Mississippi where Pa was the doctor for the town and for the people at the big plantations out along the river and for the dirt farmers, too. We weren't rich, but we were comfortable. Our house was a two-story one of white wood, and Pa saw to it that it was always freshly painted and the white picket fence around the garden was straight and even. In summer, that fence was covered with beautiful red roses that were his pride.

Sometimes Pa let me go with him when he went to see patients, and I liked it best when we went to the great big houses. I could dream about myself living on a huge plantation, coming down one of those curving staircases in a great flowing gown. I used to sit in the entryway and wait for Pa and vow that someday I, too, would live like that. I surely never meant to live in a two-room house in East Texas!

The nicest thing about our life though was Mama. Mama was all light and laughter and pretty clothes and parties. She

9

was kind of tall, with lots of blonde hair she piled high on her head. She always wore dainty, pretty clothes, like pink dresses that showed off her pale skin. After she got sick, she got even prettier. Her skin seemed so pale you could almost see through it and her cheeks were real rosy. Pa told me later that was what consumption did to people.

Before that, Mama used to fill our house with ladies of an afternoon, but then she'd have it all quiet and welcoming for Pa when he came home. Pa didn't much like parties, the way Mama did, but he adored Mama and sometimes he'd go with her of an evening because it made him happy to see her enjoying herself.

I loved them both very much, in different ways, but sometimes I felt like an outsider, like they had a secret that I didn't know. Those were the times I wished I had brothers and sisters, but now here I was about to inherit a ready-made brother, and the idea sounded horrible to me. It wasn't only that I didn't want to share Pa, it was that everything seemed wrong anyway, and I couldn't see that letting Luke live with us would do anything but make it worse.

Taking Luke in with us wouldn't bring back the past, and that was all I really wanted. I wanted to close my eyes and go back to the days before The War, before Pa was wounded and came limping home with that awful, haunted look in his eyes. He didn't talk much about The War; in fact, he refused when people asked him. I thought he was a hero, having fought for the Confederacy, and would be glad to tell all loyal Southerners about it, but Pa told me, just once, that war was too horrible to talk about. There was nothing ever to be proud of, he said, not even if it was for the cause of the Confederacy.

Pa was still limping around on crutches when Mama began to get so sick, and I could tell he was worried about her. Like I said, she got paler and paler, and she coughed a lot and didn't have much energy. Matter of fact, she lay on the fainting couch most of the day. I remember one afternoon when Pa went to check on her. I stood outside the door, listening, and I heard her say the words "cough" and "blood" in that funny voice she had in those days, like she was always out of breath.

"It's bad, isn't it, Theodore?"

"No, Julie, don't worry. You'll be fine soon."

Maybe that was when Pa made up his mind we would head west, though I think he knew even then it was too late. The thing that really made us pack up and go wasn't Mama. It was a Northern gentleman, so he said, named Mr. Blocker. By that time, Reconstruction was on us and men from the North had come to tell us how to run our town. Pa was well enough to get out of the house, then, and he spent his days helping wherever he was needed . . . sometimes he'd care for the sick, sometimes he'd do a chore or two for a widow, even though his hip still bothered him pretty much. There weren't too many men left in Green City, except the Northerners who never helped anybody, and Pa felt like he was needed everywhere.

This particular day, Mr. Blocker came up the walk bold as you please and announced he had to see Pa. He was fat, with a red face and bald head, and I disliked him right away. When I told him Pa wasn't there, he insisted on speaking to Mama, even though I told him she was sick. Mama finally came downstairs in her dressing gown, and that man stood there and told her something awful about taxes, how we had to pay so much or they'd take our house away. He was so mean and ugly about it, he frightened Mama and she fainted right there in front of the door.

That was when Pa came home, at just the perfect moment. He must have guessed what was going on, though I didn't understand how he knew. He went straight to Mama, bent over her and listened to her breathing 'til he was sure she was all right. Then he stood up and said to this Mr. Blocker, "I'll thank you to get out of my house right now," with a kind of extra emphasis on the "right now." It was the maddest I'd ever seen Pa, but that was all he said.

Mr. Blocker muttered something about threats, but he left right quick, scurrying down the walk like he was afraid, and Pa somehow managed to carry Mama back upstairs. I still remember standing there in the hall, wishing Pa had hit that Mr. Blocker. I asked him later why he didn't, and Pa looked surprised that I had asked.

11

"Theo, Theo," he shook his head as he talked, "that would not do any good. It would only make me as low as he is . . . or worse. That's how wars start, Theo, because one side gets mad and hits first. Mr. Blocker isn't worth lowering myself."

The very next day, Pa came home with a wagon, a great big one that had four poles in each corner and a canvas stretched over them. It sure wasn't a covered wagon, like you heard people went west in, but it would keep things dry and there would be a place for Mama to be sheltered. Big as that wagon was, I remember looking at it and worrying how we would fit all our goods in. I needn't have worried. We just didn't take much at all.

Nan, our cook and housekeeper, helped us pack, all the time fussing over us and saying she'd come with us, but Pa told her no. She had a family in a shack on the edge of town, and that was where she belonged. In the end, Pa gave her most of the furniture from the house and some of Mama's good dresses. Mama just lay there and watched him sort out what would go with us and what wouldn't, and finally she closed her eyes like she didn't want to see.

Of all the beautiful furniture in that house, we only brought a chair that had belonged to Pa's mother and Mama's fainting couch. Pa arranged the couch carefully in the wagon, so Mama could lie on it all the time we traveled. Then he packed all the other stuff we could take around the couch. There were pots and pans, a few of Pa's books, one or two of my special things like the China-face doll I'd played with in happier days.

It was sad the day we left. Nan stood there and cried, and Mama hid her head in a pillow, and I sat on the seat next to Pa and looked straight ahead. Pa closed the door to the house, came down and got in the wagon after hugging Nan once, and drove away. None of us looked back. We left Green City for good and all.

Mama never questioned Pa, figuring he knew best, but I didn't understand. "Why did we have to leave, Pa?" I was nearly in tears as we rode along.

"Green City isn't a fit place to live any more, Theo."

"Couldn't we just pay the taxes?"

"No. They're illegal taxes. And if we paid them, those men would think of something else."

"But Mama's so sick . . ."

"She won't get any sicker traveling than she would if we were evicted," he said grimly. "And if she can make it out west, she might get better."

Neither of us believed that, but we lied to ourselves.

I didn't want to remember much about that long, endless trip. We bounced over muddy, rutted roads, froze in the cold rain, blistered in the sun, and all the time Mama got weaker and weaker. She never complained, and she was always brave when Pa checked on her, but all of us knew it was no good. Pa talked heartily as he could about the dry air out west and what good it would do her to be out there. I never found out where "out there" was, though I feared it was where there were wild Indians, and I thought Mama might do better any-where else. But I never found out because Mama died, and we stopped our journey.

Mama didn't even make it to the edge of Texas. She died in some little place in Louisiana, and we buried her in a burying ground there with a Romanish priest saying the prayers be-cause he was all that was around. I knew Pa didn't like that, but he wouldn't let Mama go into the ground without a ser-vice. Pa knows the name of the place where she's buried, and he says we'll go back sometime and put flowers on the grave. I doubt it, and I don't think I want to anyway.

But after that, Pa had no reason to go anywhere. He didn't need to take Mama to dry air, he couldn't go back to the house he'd walked away from, and he had me to take care of—or I had him, I wasn't sure by this time which way it was. We just kind of kept on going without knowing where we were.

And that's how I ended up in an East Texas cabin listening to the rain. When we got to Canton, Pa stopped at a place called The Clancey Inn. I didn't think it was much of a place, what with dirt floors, not even boards, in the kitchen and dining room. And the two or three meals we ate there, I spent a lot of my time looking around at the men. They looked like outlaws, I thought, though I wasn't real sure what outlaws looked like. But Pa was my standard of what gentlemen should look like, and these men weren't real neat and clean. Mamie, the cook, told me once two men got into a fight, and Mrs. Clancey pulled a pistol to make them stop. I was horrified, but Mamie thought it was a funny story and laughed so hard she cried.

Pa got to talking with Mrs. Clancey. She said they needed a doctor bad, last one had gone off to fight for the North, which I thought was scandalous. Anyway, she kept telling Pa about this doctor's cabin with all his books and medicines still there. Pa listened a long while, and then said he'd stay. I thought it was a hasty decision, not like Pa, but I guessed I understood.

For Pa, Canton was a place where he could do the one thing left that was important to him, and that was practice medicine. I guess he intended to work so hard he wouldn't have time to grieve.

We'd been in Canton less than a month, and it rained near all that time. Now things were going from bad to worse. I thought about Luke again as I reached over to blow out the lamp. Then I slept, but it wasn't a happy sleep.

2

CANTON WAS A SMALL TOWN, smaller even than Green City, and I thought it was a lot less attractive. There was a one-room log courthouse in the middle of the town square, and the streets were muddy and unkempt, with gullies in them after a good rain. A ravine ran right through the middle of town, and I wondered why a town was ever built on such an awkward spot. But then I remembered the story Pa said he'd heard from one of his patients, about how the entire town was once owned by a private citizen. It seems the surveyors made a mistake and laid out the town in the middle of someone's fields. So probably, that same sorry survey accounted for the town being built around the ravine.

The Clancey Inn was the most impressive building in town, two stories tall and painted fairly recently. There was a storekeeper, Edgeworth, whose wife was one of the few people I knew in Canton. She was always nice and talkative when I went after supplies, even if I didn't talk much myself. Canton also had a church, the butcher shop owned by a man named Jones who I thought was gruff and unfriendly, a schoolhouse, a real small bank and a livery stable. Several years before there'd been a newspaper, *The Canton Courier*, but it had disappeared during the war.

The biggest activity in Canton came when the farmers brought produce and animals to town to trade. You'd see a wagon with an old horse tied behind it and know that someone had probably filed the horse's teeth down in hopes of concealing his age and making a good sale. Mostly, they came on the day when the district court met, because there were always more people around then, and the farmers had a better chance of selling their chickens and eggs and squash and melons and what all they grew and raised.

Canton wasn't like Green City at all. There weren't any big plantations or people who had slaves, or even hired help, and who lived nice gracious lives. Everyone in Canton seemed poor to me, and as far as I could tell, they never had afternoon teas, like Mama used to, or church social suppers, or any of the wonderful things I remembered from home.

Pa kept telling me to give Canton a chance, that I'd learn to like it if I'd stop expecting it to be just like Green City. "Canton's an entirely different place, Theo, and you've got to realize that."

I realized, all right, but I didn't want to accept. Maybe I would have liked Canton better if I'd had friends there, but I hadn't had much chance to meet girls my own age since school was almost out for the year when we arrived, and the teacher told Pa to wait until the fall to send me. Besides, I'd rejected one or two offers of friendship from a couple of girls, not because I didn't want friends but mostly, I guess, because I was sunk too deep in self-pity. You can hardly be friendly when all you can think about is how unfair life is.

A girl named Lucille something came all the way to our cabin one day. "Just wanted to welcome you-all," she said, shaking her blonde head slightly. "Guess we'll be going to school together in the fall."

"Guess so," I muttered. Reluctantly, I invited her into the cabin. "Want a glass of lemonade?"

"That surely would be nice," Lucille said smiling. She was a pretty girl, smaller than me, which didn't help my feelings about her.

Over lemonade, we talked about The War, and she wanted

to know all about what it was like in Mississippi, but I told her I didn't want to talk about Mississippi.

"I can understand that," she said. "War didn't touch us here as much, and I feel sorry for you. I guess now, though, with the military government, it's liable to touch us more."

I didn't even ask what she meant by that, and after a while the conversation kind of died. Lucille said she guessed it was time for her to go, and she hoped I'd come see her and we could visit often. I told her thank you and I'd see. She really was pretty nice, even if she had the nerve to pity me, and I had to admit she had tried to be friendly. But I knew I wouldn't go see her.

Luke knew all about the incident when he moved in with us. "Hear Lucille Harrison came out to see you," he said.

"What if she did?"

"Nothing. I thought it was nice of her, but she says you didn't seem too friendly."

"I was friendly," I said defensively. What business of Luke's was it anyway?

Within one week, my dislike for Luke Widman turned to pure hate. For one thing, he was never discouraged, unhappy, sad, or in one of those black moods like I got in all the time. 'Course not much later, I saw him real upset. But at first, he was happy most all the time and nothing, not even me, upset him. And he knew how to do everything. I longed to discover one thing Luke was totally ignorant about.

He fixed the door on the necessary house so it didn't swing

like it was about to fall off its hinges, and he chinked the worst of the cracks in the wall in Pa's study and told Pa he'd fix the shingles on the roof. Pa was delighted. Another thing Luke knew all about, so he said, was hunting and fishing. He promised Pa he'd bring food for us, but I didn't believe him. He proved me wrong.

I wouldn't have hated Luke if I hadn't been really mad at myself. Deep down, I guess I knew I was the only one who could make things go right for me. But there I was, awash in self-pity and waiting for the world to change. Meanwhile nothing I did toward housekeeping came out right. My cooking didn't improve, I never could keep the cabin clean, and Pa's shirts generally looked as though a dog had chewed on them before he put them on. And it took me longer to do a thing poorly than it did for most women to do it right. I never got through, because there was always some chore waiting to be done as soon as I finished whatever I was doing.

Pa never once complained about my failures, but I was depressed by them. Once I overheard Luke telling Pa that it was his belief that you had to be a survivor in this world, and I guess that was what I hated about Luke Widman. He was a survivor. His mother dead, his pa gone off and left him, yet Luke went along liking each day, getting things done and getting them done right.

On the other hand, I was less and less sure I was a survivor. The primary qualification seemed to me that you did well at whatever circumstances life threw at you, and I seemed to be doing poorly. I figured that if I didn't lick this housekeeping business, I could never move forward to anything else. I'd just be stuck trying to be a housekeeper, and failing, the rest of my life. Luke, though, he was going to move forward, probably to be a doctor someday.

One morning I went out to hang clothes, a chore I despised, and found him digging in the ground, using one of our table spoons.

"Luke, what are you doing with that good spoon?" I tried to let him know I disapproved by the tone in my voice.

"Diggin' worms," he said as though there were nothing wrong with it. "Ground's real soft, still wet. Won't hurt the spoon none."

"But it's a spoon we eat with!"

"I'll wash it good." He plainly implied that I was making a fuss about nothing, but as usual my fuss failed to anger him. "Here, I'll help you with those clothes, then you can help me dig."

"No, thanks." I marched indignantly toward the clothesline. I wasn't about to dig worms. Back home in Mississippi, the little slave children had dug for worms, but none of the girls I knew ever went fishing, let alone dug around in the ground looking for slimy old worms.

I pulled the first wet shirt out of the basket and started untangling it. One wet sleeve flopped in my face and I nearly dropped the whole thing in the dirt. Behind me, there was a soft chuckle which I ignored.

Still, it was the kind of day when staying angry is impossible. We'd had sunny, gorgeous days ever since that heavy rain the night of Luke's arrival. This particular day, you'd never know there was such a thing as a cloud, and the temperature was just right, not too hot nor too cold. It was spring at its best, and I loved it. My enjoyment of the weather was shattered by a comment that came from behind me.

"That sheet ain't never gonna' dry if you leave it bunched like that."

"I'm not through."

He was silent while I finished with the rest of the wash, but I could tell he was watching me, waiting 'til I was done. Finally, I had the last shirt up, and I headed for the house with the basket.

"Wanna go fishing?"

"Fishing!"

"Sure. I'm gonna catch some bass for supper. Least I hope I am."

19

Now I no more wanted to go fishing than I wanted to stay home and scrub that dirty board floor one more time, but I really did want to be outside. I was plain bored with doing housework all the time, and being inside and not having any fun and not having any company. Not that Luke Widman was company, but maybe it would be better than being alone.

"Wait 'til I see if Pa needs me. I might just go and watch."

"Just watch?"

"That's all," I said firmly.

Pa looked kind of glad when I said I might go. I don't know whether it was because he, too, thought I was inside too much or because he wanted Luke and me to turn out friends. We sure hadn't headed that way so far. Least I hadn't.

Luke led the way down the road, away from town, carrying his bucket of worms—he had a powerful lot of them—two fishing poles, and a sack that held I didn't know what. We followed the road quite a piece, past great stands of trees where the ground was covered with a tangle of weeds and bushes and past an occasional field, cleared for planting. Most of East Texas, I had already found, was a jungle of uncleared forest and when little patches of it were cleared, the soil was often pure sand and clay.

Without a word, Luke struck off across a small field that had once been cleared and was beginning to grow over again. He headed directly towards a distant line of trees.

"Watch where you're walking," he threw over his shoulder. "Snakes might be stirring in this warm weather."

Snakes! I was ready to turn and go back that minute, but something, pride I guess, kept me from it. I wasn't going to let him frighten me. But I watched where I walked real carefully, even though it was hard to see the ground sometimes through the grass and weeds.

The line of trees proved to be a woods, but Luke walked like he knew where he was going, picking his way around bramble bushes and broken trees, and even holding a branch for me now and then. We probably hadn't gone far, though it seemed like a long way to me, when all of a sudden there was a big pond in front of us. Trees grew right up to the edge, so that it seemed to me the water just suddenly materialized out of nowhere.

"This here's Web Turner's stock tank," Luke explained. "Crotchety old man lives over the other side there,"—he gestured across the water, but I could see no house—"likes to be left alone all the time. But he told me I could fish here." Without any further comment, Luke settled himself on the bank and began arranging his pole, reaching for a worm.

"Here's your pole."

"I'm not going to fish."

"Suit yourself."

I sat gingerly at the water's edge, having looked around for snakes and any other varmints before I sat down in the dryest, cleanest spot I could find. The sun was warm, making me a little drowsy and uncomfortable like I wanted to stretch out and sleep but couldn't. Across the water, dogwood and redbud trees dotted the still-bare woods with dainty touches of pink and white, and the water in between was perfectly still, so that it mirrored the blooming trees. Once a duck swam around a curve in the bank, took one look at us and squawked indignantly before disappearing again. His squawk echoed clearly across the water.

Luke broke the silence to tell me there were gators living in the water. Like a dummy, I asked, "What's a gator?"

"Alligators," he said with exasperation.

"Alligators?" That was definitely worse than snakes, and I was ready to run.

"Won't bother you if you don't bother them," he said superiorly.

There was silence again for a while, but as the sun warmed me inside and out, I felt like talking. "Tell me," I asked, "about this man—what's his name? Turner?"

Luke looked at me quizzically for a minute, then said, "Web's okay. Folks don't understand about him. They think he used to help runaway slaves get up North."

"How awful!" I said. Where I came from helping slaves was almost worse than murder.

"Naw, it ain't awful, if that's what you believe is right. But I don't know if he done it or not."

I ignored his grammar. "But they weren't his property. It wasn't right to help them get away."

Luke looked sorry he had brought it up. "I told you it's just 21 a rumor. I ain't gonna argue about it. And if you don't hush, no fish'll come within a mile of us."

I was silent again, feeling rebuffed. It was a long while before Luke broke the silence with a yell, "I got a bite!"

I watched the end of his pole bend and dance as the fish struggled and Luke began slowly to lift it out of the water. The only way he could pull the fish in was to stand up and walk away from the water, holding his pole as straight as possible. But silly as he looked, he had caught a good fish. I didn't know much about the size of fish, but this one looked like it might have enough meat on it to be worth cooking.

"It's a keeper," he said, his face glowing with pleasure.

I stared a minute. It wasn't the fish that was remarkable. It was the look of pure joy on Luke's face. He looked like he'd really done something that made him happy. Very carefully, he unhooked the fish and attached it to a line he got out of his mysterious sack. Then he tied the line to a tree and gently put the fish back in the water.

"What're you doing?" I was certain that he was going to lose his fish after all.

"Got to keep him fresh 'til we go home."

It was another of those things Luke knew, just plain knew, and I didn't.

I watched for a while longer, then as casually as I could said, "If you bait a hook for me, I think I'll try."

He didn't laugh or anything, but he meant it when he said, "If you want to fish, you got to bait your own hook."

There were lots of things I could have done, like pouting and making a face or saying, "Oh, please," or just getting mad and walking away. But I didn't do any of those things, though I'm not sure why. Back home in Mississippi I would have expected someone to do it for me, but that was before. I'd learned to do a lot of other things and maybe this was just another one. Besides, I wasn't going to let Luke Widman show me up.

I baited the hook, though I had to bite my tongue to keep from saying "Ick" at the least. But I never let on that it bothered me, and he pretended not to watch.

Luke caught five fish that day, and I got two, one of them a

23

good-sized one, big enough, he said, for the frying pan. And he did help me take mine off the hook.

"So you don't tear it to pieces," he explained.

It was late afternoon, with long grey shadows falling through the woods, by the time we headed back, Luke swinging the line of fish in one hand and the bucket, now nearly empty, in the other. I held two poles straight out in front of me until he suggested they'd ride better over my shoulder.

We had fish for dinner that night, and Pa was real pleased.

"Theo caught some, too," Luke told him, and I saw Pa's eyebrows go up.

"Theo! I didn't know you were a fisherman."

"Luke showed me." Some of the pride in my catch kind of disappeared, and I was afraid next I'd have to admit that Luke had to show me how to cook the fish, too. I hated having him teach me how to do things.

"Luke," I said, "get your elbows off the table, and raise your food to your face, don't lower your face to your plate." His table manners were awful, and I always wanted to correct him. I wasn't sure why I'd chosen that particular moment to comment, but I saw the first look of anger I'd ever seen on Luke's face.

Pa just said quietly, "I'll help Luke with his manners, Theo."

The incident of the griddle cakes was even worse. At least, Luke didn't laugh at me about baiting the fishhook, and he really tried to boost me by telling Pa so carefully that I'd caught one of our dinner fish, too. The griddle cakes were totally different, but I guess by then I'd made him mad.

Now I wasn't much of a cook. Pa and I had some pretty

disastrous meals since we'd set up housekeeping together. But Pa was patient, and he never complained, though I know some nights he must have been pretty hungry. 'Course, he couldn't help much, because he didn't know anything about cooking himself.

Back in Green City, I'd never learned to cook because Mama didn't think I needed to. In her view, there would always be Nan or someone to do it for me. Ladies didn't have to slave over a hot stove. The kitchen was one of my favorite places. I'd sit and watch Nan for hours, and I suppose I'd learned a little. When I was real small, she'd let me crack eggs and stir things and, of course, lick the spoon.

Just before we left Nan back in Mississippi, I'd even asked her to tell me how to make some things. I could see a lot of cooking ahead of me and, much as I resented it, I thought I best be prepared. So she told me in her own way.

Nan was a pinch and taste cook—add a pinch of salt or a handful of flour, taste, then add salt or flour according to how it tasted and felt. A beginner can hardly do that, but I tried, and sometimes Pa was downright complimentary about my cooking.

One day when Luke hadn't been with us too long, I decided to make griddle cakes. Pa had a big jug of molasses given to him for taking care of the man who owned the molasses mill, and we could pour that over the cakes. I got out my notes from Nan and followed her instructions religiously, even trying to figure how big her handful of flour was to mine. Mixing up the batter went okay, but Nan hadn't said one word about how to cook them.

Without telling him what I wanted to do, I told Luke to stoke up the stove. He muttered, "Yes sir!" under his breath as he went out, but I ignored him.

The stove was a solid cast-iron affair that sat on little legs and had a door in the front where you threw in the wood. On top there were two places to set pots and a griddle. 'Course there was no such thing as low and high heat. Once you got it stoked up, it just burned one way—hot!

Luke got the wood for the stove, and I waited a bit for it to heat up. But the fire hadn't got a good start when I went ahead and poured batter on the griddle. It was a disaster. First of all, I poured too much batter on and it nearly ran down into the stove, prevented only by hasty mopping on my part. By the time I got it under control, the fire was much hotter and I thought it was time to turn the cakes. But try as I might, I could not get that gummy, sticky mess off the griddle.

Of course, that was when Luke came in. There I was, scraping frantically at those cakes which were now burning and smelling, with batter burned onto the stove where my mopping and wiping had failed. My temper was as frazzled as the hair which hung in strings in my face. I brushed it away with a floury hand, turning my brown hair grey, and looked up to see him standing there, watching, grinning like mad.

"Didn't get the griddle hot enough," he finally said.

"Oh, thanks." I hoped he caught my sarcasm.

"Better start over again. Here, let me have that." He took the griddle out of my hand, took it outside and somehow got rid of the mess. Angry and frustrated, I stood where I was, rooted to the spot in front of the stove.

"Bet you don't even know how to clean a hot skillet," he said disgustedly when he came in. I just glared but he went on talking without seeming to notice my look. "Throw it into the dirt. Cools it off and the dirt kind of scrubs it."

I forgot to be silent and angry as I echoed incredulously, "Dirt?"

"Oh, I washed it after that." He threw me another black look, as if to say, "How dumb do you think I am?" Then he began to give orders. "Here, you get the table ready. I'll do the griddle cakes."

I was furious but I obeyed. And he did do the cakes. He knew just when the griddle was hot enough, just when to flip the cakes—later he told me it was by bubbles on the uncooked side—and, in short, just how to cook delicious griddle cakes.

But he did the unforgivable. He laughed at me—in front of Pa. "Never saw a girl who couldn't cook griddle cakes," he went on, carried away with his own humor.

I burned with embarrassment, and it wasn't much help

when Pa put a casual arm around my shoulders and said, "She'll learn. I've got a lot of confidence in Theo."

Sometimes I was so lonely, it was like a big ache. Pa wasn't much company, and most times I thought Luke was worse than none. Oh, Pa and Luke talked of an evening, but somehow my part seemed to be to sit and listen. I remembered the days when I felt like the center of a family, not an invisible person who sat on the side and wasn't part of the conversation, and I wanted the past back.

Some evenings, Luke talked about his family, how his pa had just kept moving west, farming first this patch of land and then that and never making much of a living. "He always said he had a wandering streak in his soul," Luke told Pa. "But I guess they loved each other very much, at least once long ago before Ma got sick and all. She never complained about Pa's moves, even when she'd tell me stories of the places we'd lived. We'd been in Van Zandt County near six years, and that's a record. 'Course I don't remember too many of the other places."

Luke went on and told how his father's family were still back in West Virginia—grandparents and uncles that Luke had never seen or known.

"Would you like to know your relatives, Luke? Family's important to a man."

"Yeah," Luke agreed slowly, "I would. But right now, I got family right here."

"Yes, son, you do." I squirmed and busied myself with my sewing, but Pa went right on to ask, "What about your mother's people?"

"She never talked about them. Pa told me once they for . . . for . . . oh, they told her she couldn't marry him, but she did it anyway, and she wouldn't talk about it. I guess, from what Pa said, they had more money than Pa's folks, and I know Ma had more schooling. She used to tell me how important school was, but Pa, he always said I could learn what I needed out in the world. He said school was a waste of time."

"I agree with your mother," Pa said quietly but with great determination.

"Well, Pa said experience was the best teacher. That's why I thought it was smart to be with you to learn to be a doctor—I'd get experience."

"Why do you want to be a doctor?"

"Because of Ma. Because she should have had a doctor and there wasn't one, and because . . . long before she got sick, Ma used to talk about my being a doctor. It was like a dream of hers . . . I used to think maybe her pa was a doctor."

This conversation and others like it did little to ease my loneliness, because neither of them talked to me. The growing closeness between Pa and Luke left me out. Once I tried to enter the conversation by asking how Luke's father could just ride away like that, but Luke muttered, "You wouldn't understand, Theo," and went on talking to Pa.

I longed for Mama, not only her laughter and happiness but her listening ear. Mama used to have serious conversations with me, just like Pa was now having with Luke, and she never laughed at any of my problems or questions. If only I could talk to her now I could pour out all my hatred of housework and my loneliness . . . but that was a circle in my thoughts, because if Mama were here, I wouldn't be lonely.

The person I most wanted to see, besides Mama, was my best friend back home, Amelia May. Just talking to her would help, I thought, and so one fine afternoon, I took pad and pencil out to an old stump behind the cabin and began to write Amelia May a letter. Of course, I improved Canton some and wasn't quite truthful about the size of our new home, nor its appearance, but I did tell the whole truth about missing my mother and my friends and being homesick and lonely.

I'd write a little, then stare at the wisteria bush that bloomed near the door and made the air heavy with perfume, or I'd count the lazy clouds that floated across the sky, or count the freckles that blossomed on my arms, and then I'd write some more. I was in one of my staring periods when I heard a wagon approach, but I didn't pay too much attention. It was probably just another patient.

Pa's practice had been good since we'd come to Canton. They really did need a doctor in the worst way, and Pa was kept busy treating fevers in children and cuts and wounds in big and little citizens. Already he'd had two cases of diphtheria—both patients had survived, thank goodness—and some scarlet fever and chicken pox. There was a midwife to help with the birthing, but she asked Pa's advice a lot of the time, and all told, he was pretty busy. Sometimes, he was away a lot, going from house to house and learning his way around Van Zandt County in a hurry, but other times people came to his study to see him. So I just thought this was another patient come to the house.

When I heard Pa call, I knew it was a patient but not a regular one.

"Theo! Come here, please!"

Back home when Pa took me on house calls, he never let me near his patients. If he ever needed help, he took Nan's husband, Jake. It wouldn't have been ladylike for me or Mama to see our neighbors or acquaintances when they were patients, let alone help Pa treat them. But a time or two as we traveled across the South, Pa needed help, and there was no one else. It was hard for me, but I learned to soothe a patient while Pa sewed up a bad wound, hold a head while he extracted a tooth, even when need be apply pressure to staunch bleeding. I knew from the tone in his voice this time that he needed me to help with a patient.

Luke materialized as I rounded the corner onto the dogtrot, and he followed me into the study. Jones, the butcher from town, sat in a straight wooden chair, one hand wrapped

in a bloody rag and held straight up in the air. A rough tour-
niquet had been fashioned of another rag and a stick and applied just above his elbow. He looked a little shocked, like he
was surprised an accident had happened to him, but he managed to nod politely at me.

"Mr. Jones has had an accident with a meat cleaver, Theo.
I'll try to save his thumb by repair, but I will need you to help
control the bleeding so I can see what I'm doing." He noticed
Luke. "Luke, you can hold the lamp steady."

Luke was already looking a little pale. "Lamp? It's still light
out."

"I need all the light I can get," Pa explained patiently, while
he spread a clean cloth on one edge of the desk and laid out
cotton thread, needle and scissors.

I went out and got a basin of clean water—Pa always said it
was the best disinfectant—and more rags.

Pa unwrapped the bandage first, revealing that Mr. Jones
had nearly cut his right thumb off at the base. One quick
glance told me, though, that he had by some miracle missed
the bone. Mr. Jones had looked the other way when Pa unwrapped his thumb, but I heard Luke gasp. Pa paid no attention but motioned for me to put clean rags all around the
wound. Then, with a quick motion, he released the tourni-
quet and blood spurted from the wound, high enough that a
great red patch began to spread on Luke's shirt. He looked
down at it in amazement and opened his mouth to protest, realizing just in time that this was not the moment to complain.

Pa had to work quick to get that bleeding stopped. He used
a pair of forceps to find the artery and clamp it, then I held
the clamp tight while he tied off the artery which was still
spurting a small stream of blood. With my other hand, I was
fighting a losing battle to mop up the blood and keep the
wound clear enough so that Pa could see what he was doing.
Finally, he got the bleeding stopped and I got enough blood
cleaned up that he could begin the much slower job of repairing the slash across the thumb.

"You're a lucky man, Mr. Jones. Bones are intact and no
major nerves or tendons appear to be cut. The blood made it
look worse than it is."

"Thanks, Doc," his patient said weakly.

My job was about over, except for a little swabbing. I looked away while Pa snipped and stitched, but I guess Luke didn't look away, because suddenly the light moved and I looked up to see Luke headed out the door.

Pa didn't say a thing, just moved the lamp over as close as he could set it and went on with his work. I couldn't help smiling grimly. Luke and I were even now.

If I'd been Luke Widman and left the room that way, I'd have been so mortified there'd been no dragging me back. But not Luke. He reappeared a few minutes later, looking a little humble maybe but not as though he'd lost every ounce of his pride. Without a word, he picked up the lamp and held it close to where Pa was working. By this time, Pa didn't need me any more, and I was cutting a clean bandage and waiting till Pa asked for it. Mr. Jones' hand was finally almost sewn up.

"That's going to be stiff, but you can probably use it."

"Figured," was the patient's answer. "Know you done the best you could, Doc. You send these young'uns to the store and I'll have some good meat for them."

We would be grateful, I knew, for meat was rare on our table these days. Pa, of course, didn't hunt, which was how lots of families got meat, and we didn't raise cattle or hogs. We didn't even have our own chickens, though Luke insisted we needed them.

Pa said appropriate thanks and gave Jones instructions on taking care of his hand, explaining that he had to watch carefully for red streaks heading up his hand which would be a sign of infection and meant he had to come see Pa immediately.

"Infection?" he asked, obviously alarmed.

"There's only a slim chance," Pa assured him. "We cleaned it pretty well, but I just wanted to warn you. You come back in a week and we'll see about taking those stitches out."

Jones got back in the wagon where, all this time, his oldest son had been sitting, waiting, afraid, I suppose, to hear what the doctor said or see what he did.

While I cleaned up, Pa and Luke had a talk, but it didn't go anything like I expected.

"Sorry I disappointed you, sir."

"Happens to everyone, Luke. Get a little sick, did you?"

That nervy Luke Widman didn't deny it or anything, just stood there and said, "Yes, sir, first time I seen anything like that. 'Course I've taken care of animals that were hurt and all, but . . . well, it's different when it's a person."

"Yes it is, Luke, and that's an important thing to remember. You needn't feel too bad about what happened today . . . matter of fact, it's a good sign."

"It is? I was kind of worried I couldn't, well, that it meant, you know . . . I wouldn't be able to be a doctor."

"Not strong enough in the stomach, eh? No, I think on the other hand it shows that you have the compassion it takes to be a really good physician."

Now I knew full good and well Luke Widman didn't know what the word "compassion" meant, but he never let on, just stood there smiling like always.

Finally, he said, "I'll try to see it don't happen again."

Pa corrected him automatically. "Doesn't happen, Luke. And it won't, believe me."

I wasn't even with Luke after all. In disgust, I picked up the things I had to wash and left, ignoring Luke, who asked "Can I help?"

"You could have ten minutes ago," I threw over my shoulder.

To my surprise, Luke followed me. "Don't you want to say anything smart about my getting sick?" he asked in a taunting voice.

"You sound like you're proud of it," I accused.

"I am not! But if I were you, I wouldn't be very proud of the way I was acting, either."

"Look who's talking! You can't even eat a meal without spilling your food."

"And you can't go a minute without criticizing me or correcting me. You're like a hawk, waiting for a rabbit to make a mistake."

"I don't have to wait long," I said smugly.

Luke walked to the edge of the dogtrot, stood there a

minute, and then stepped into the road. I really couldn't understand what he was doing, but he stopped and picked up a huge stone from the road. Then, with all the force he could muster, he heaved it as far as possible. It wasn't the kind of throw kids use when they skip rocks in a river or toss pebbles at a tree. It was an angry, almost violent gesture. Then he turned and came back on the porch.

"All right, Theo. Let's start over."

"Start over?"

"Yes. I know he's your pa, and you don't want to share him, but, Theo, I'm not going to leave here just because you're jealous."

I stared silently. His words hit close to home, and I didn't know what to say.

"I think we can be friends, Theo. Can't we try?"

"How?"

"You stop criticizing me."

"And you stop making me look so dumb."

"Deal."

He held out his hand to shake on it, and I hesitated just a minute. If I followed my instinct and turned away, I'd be breaking the deal first off. But shaking his hand was awful hard for me.

I know Pa heard us outside, but he never came out of his study. All along, he'd been kind of the peacemaker between us, and I guess he thought we finally had to work it out for ourselves. Trouble is, I didn't know if we had worked it out or just patched things up temporarily.

3

L UKE AND I continued in an armed truce, with a couple of peaceful interludes, for a month or more. He still teased unmercifully about my housekeeping—"Can I help you find the stove, Theo?" or "Where'd you get this chicken? Find it run over in the road?"—and I still bristled in anger each time. But I was learning to hold my own, and I left his grammar and table manners to Pa. I still didn't like having him with us, and I still thought he was pushy and insufferable, but I tolerated him.

Then a hint of trouble to come in Van Zandt County, serious trouble, made the squabble between us fade into the background of my thoughts. All along I had thought Van Zandt County was a pretty peaceful place, not exactly prosperous, but peaceful. The War began to seem long ago and far away. Not too many men from Canton and around there had gone to war. I guess most of them proved hardship to avoid the draft. And there were no slaveowners or big plantations with men who would fight willingly for the sake of the South. I even got the impression that more than a few men around sympathized with the North. But mostly, they just didn't want to be involved.

Van Zandt County was sometimes mockingly called a Free State, and Luke told me a story about why. It seems that before The War, lots of Southerners came to Texas looking for a place to hide their slaves. One time, one of them stopped in Canton and somebody asked if he was bringing slaves to Van Zandt County. He said he'd as soon leave them up North in a free state because he looked all around and didn't see any other slaves. And there weren't any. Van Zandt County didn't have as much at stake in the war as people back in Mississippi and in other southern states.

Anyway, The War hadn't made near the difference in the lives of the people here that it had back home and neither had Reconstruction or the military government. We heard awful tales from other parts of Texas, and Pa tried to explain to me how humiliating the occupation was to Texans. He even told me about General Sheridan, said most folks said he was the one who forced General Lee to surrender at Appomattox—that didn't make me like him at all! Pa said he was a dedicated soldier who never took pity on anyone, so I guessed he didn't pity the Texans he was in charge of. I was kind of glad to hear he was short and funny looking rather than tall, dark and handsome like soldiers and heroes should be. But General Sheridan and his military occupation government seemed a million miles away to me. I found out I was wrong, by eavesdropping.

Well, it wasn't exactly eavesdropping, but Mayor Clintlock came to see Pa and after they closed the door to the study, they got to talking real loud. At least, the mayor did; talking loud wasn't something Pa did. But I got curious. Why would they close the door when it was bound to be beastly hot in that little, airless room? And why was the mayor yelling?

Broom in hand, I sneaked across the dogtrot and put my ear real close to the door. If they came out, I'd just start to sweep real quick. Meanwhile, I listened and could make out some of what they said. I heard the mayor shout the hated name of Sheridan, and the words "free state" and "we won't stand for it" and I could hear a soft murmur when Pa answered.

"You've got to . . ." He seemed to be threatening Pa.

I remembered the reconstruction man who'd scared Mama and Pa's reaction to that. I began to worry some. Could I, I wondered, inch the door open without them knowing?

"Theo, what in land's sake are you doing there?" Luke came up behind me, talking as loud as he could.

"Shh!" I whirled around, putting a finger to my lips.

"Don't tell me to shush! You shouldn't be listening at your pa's door."

Disgusted, I pulled him by the arm until we were clear of the house. "I wasn't listening . . . well, not exactly . . . Mr. Clintlock's yelling at Pa . . ."

That changed his tune completely. "Yelling at your pa? What about?"

The closeness between Pa and Luke caused me much concern and, let's face it, much jealousy. But right now that closeness and Luke's fierce adoration of Pa worked to my advantage. Luke would have fought bear for Pa, let alone someone who was hollering at him.

"That's what I was trying to find out," I said indignantly.

Luke took charge immediately, or tried to. "You go on and sweep while I listen," he commanded.

"I will not! We'll both listen."

"Theo, if we stand here arguing about it all day, we'll never find out what's going on."

"You're right," I said and marched right back to the door to Pa's room. After all, I was the one who had discovered the yelling, and I wasn't going to let Luke take charge. It was like the awfulness of Pa's being yelled at belonged to me, and I wouldn't share. He was my pa, not Luke's.

"We've got to arm ourselves. Don't you see, Burford, we're in danger from all sides . . . Sheridan's military troops, those free blacks, and now, this thing called the Ku Klux Klan." Mr. Clintlock seemed to be pleading with Pa.

"Mr. Clintlock," Pa said, still real soft, "if you'd seen war as I've seen it, you'd have no desire ever to give a rifle to another human being. We have to approach problems with reason and intelligence, not violence."

"What good's reason and intelligence going to do us?"

37

I knew that question would pain Pa, because the answer should be obvious, but he was polite when he said to Mr. Clintlock, "If you have serious complaints, present them to Sheridan."

"He hates Texas! He won't listen. Haven't you heard what they're quoting from him?"

"That if he owned Texas and Hell, he'd live in Hell and rent out Texas?" Pa chuckled a little. "Yes, I heard. But he's in command. He has to listen, and he will. Surely he's a fair man."

"I doubt that. Besides, it's not that we really have had any trouble yet. It's just that we've got to be prepared. Look what's happening to the south of us . . . blacks rising up in the fields, killings, then the Klan begins to ride. They've been on some of their midnight trips as close as Tyler."

"But they have no reason to come to Canton, do they? As I understand it, the Klan is most active down around San Augustine where there are so many free Negroes, some of them . . . ah, as you say, unruly."

It sounded like Mr. Clintlock was driven by fear, and Pa wasn't going to get too far reasoning with him. He nearly screamed at Pa, "Those people are wild! You can't reason with them, and you can't tell where or what they'll do next. They're likely to get it in their heads that you or I have been helping blacks. Think of that, Burford—the Klan could come visit you some night. They'd be wrong, of course, but they don't care. We must be prepared!" It was a long speech, even for Mayor Clintlock.

"I certainly agree that each citizen should be prepared to defend his home and family, but an army, Mr. Clintlock? An independent, illegal army?"

"I have lots of support for this in town."

"I'm afraid you must." Pa sounded sad.

"It won't go well, Burford, when people find out you're opposed to us."

"Ah, now, Mr. Clintlock, I'm not opposed, at least not in the sense of taking any action. But I will do nothing to support you either."

Luke and I looked at each other, each with the same thought. Mr. Clintlock would be coming out in a moment, and I better start sweeping. I jerked the broom upright to begin a vigorous attack on the dogtrot. Only the broom caught in Luke's pants leg, and when I pulled hard, I jerked his feet out from underneath him. He let out an indignant yelp as he crashed to the floor, and I couldn't help laughing. Thinking it was funny to see Luke in a tangle on the floor, I pretended to sweep right around him.

"I thought you said to be quiet," I reminded him.

Luke got up slowly, brushing off his clothes and rubbing one knee where he'd landed hard. "Theo," he began . . .

"Now, Luke, it was an accident," I protested.

"Some accident," he muttered, "Can't even manage a broom, let alone a stove."

I was tempted to swat him with the broom and even raised it menacingly, but just then Pa's door opened, and he and Mayor Clintlock came out.

Mayor Arley Clintlock was also the owner of the bank in Canton, and he always dressed the part, in a suit with a white starched collar on his shirt and a proper bow tie. He carried a little round hat in his hand, and altogether he looked dapper and out of place, since no one else in Canton ever dressed like that. Mr. Clintlock took banking very serious, I supposed.

"Luke! Theo! What are you two doing?" Pa looked at us with disapproval.

Luke rushed in to answer before I could open my mouth. I guess he was afraid of what I might say. "I was about to help Theo with the housework, sir, but we got all tangled with the broom. Matter of fact, she tripped me with it." He threw me a black look. By this time, I had lowered the broom and was leaning on it.

"I would think," Pa said, "that the two of you could manage some simple chores without tangling with each other." He turned away to walk Mr. Clintlock to his buggy.

Luke disappeared too, still angry at me, I guess, and I was left alone with my broom to reflect on the fact that the truce between us had really done little to improve things. Our bickering reflected the desperate fear each of us felt, the need to be the one closest to Pa. Poor Pa, neither of us thought about what he needed.

Luke was still in a black mood and not talking to me at supper that night.

"Luke, I'm sorry about this afternoon." I thought that was enough apology. After all, it hadn't been such a big thing, and he had gotten to hear what they said.

"It's all right," he said, not even looking at me.

Things didn't get any better when Pa came in. "Luke, do you know why Mr. Clintlock called on me today?"

"No, sir." Luke, who always looked a person direct in the eye, looked anywhere but at Pa.

"Luke." There was a command in the tone.

"Maybe I got an idea . . . just an idea, though."

"Luke, do you know what's going on in town?"

"Well," he admitted reluctantly, "I have been listening here and there."

"As soon as I've had my supper, we'll talk about it."

I served Pa a silent supper that night. Luke went outside to do something—just be out of the room, I guess—and Pa ate without a word. I busied myself tidying up after dinner, but I was really curious to hear what Pa would say. It hadn't occurred to me that I wouldn't get to hear, but that's exactly what happened.

"Luke, come into my study," Pa called out through the door into the night, and back came a faint "Yes, sir."

Pa turned to me. "Theo, excuse us, please. We need to have a talk, man-to-man."

I was left out once again, and in my hurt, I really slammed

pots and pans around as I washed the dishes. But another feeling crept in beside my hurt, a feeling of foreboding, like trouble was coming. If I hadn't already nearly been caught eavesdropping once that day, I'd have crept over to listen at Pa's door.

Luke told me later about their conversation, but only after I begged and pleaded and nagged until he could stand it no longer.

"Theo Burford," he said disgustedly, after I followed him to the woodpile, "you're an awful pest. And you're making a big deal about nothing." Luke took an extra hard swing at the wood and tried to ignore me.

"I just want to know," I said stubbornly. "It's not fair for you and Pa to have secrets."

"Secrets! We ain't got no secrets. Your pa just wanted to know how many men are involved in what Mr. Clintlock was talking about and how organized they are and all. And I told him what I know."

"And?"

"And," he said exasperatedly, "he told me why it was wrong and how dangerous it could be and how strongly he feels about it."

"Did you argue?"

"Why should we argue? It wasn't a question of right or wrong. We were, well, we were just trading information."

It didn't sound like enough of a conversation to lock me out of a closed room, and I was kind of disappointed.

Pa was away more and more seeing to patients in the far edges of the county and beyond. It wasn't unusual for him to have to go ten miles to check on Mrs. Bagwell and her constipation or Mrs. Newell with her newborn baby or see to it that the young Henderson boy stayed off his broken leg. Pa wasn't even home for dinner every night and sometimes there were nights he didn't get home at all until morning. Those were the times I was real grateful for Luke, even though I never would have told him.

Of course, more times than I liked Pa took Luke with him, and I guess Luke's medical education was progressing well. He had replaced me as Pa's assistant and companion, not that I was ever much of a physician's helper. But going with Pa on house calls, like I had done since my earliest days, had given me a special place in his affections, or so I thought. Now Luke went with him. I don't think Pa realized how much that hurt me. He'd say, "Theo, you busy with that wash? I'll just take Luke with me," and they'd be gone before I could protest.

Luke had overcome his squeamishness, just as Pa said he would. I'd seen him help Pa stitch up a wound a time or two, and he never again had to leave the room. Matter of fact, sometimes I suspected Luke thought he was the doctor.

"Doesn't Mr. Earp need some Dovers' pills?" he'd ask, or "Shouldn't old Mrs. Fix be in bed?"

Pa never seemed put out that Luke tried to do his business for him. He'd discuss Luke's suggestions and tell him why they were wrong. And Luke listened real carefully every time Pa talked to him. He liked doctoring, he really did, and he'd lost none of his ambition to apprentice himself.

Sometimes they'd be discussing a case when they came in from a house call.

"That lady's just plain worn out, Luke."

"I guess," Luke agreed. "She sure looked old and tired."

"Yes, she did. Did you notice how dry her skin was, like paper? Sure sign of poor health. And her heart was weak. She's more like a woman of seventy than forty. Just worn out before her time." Pa shook his head sadly.

"Why'd you prescribe honey?"

Pa grinned a little at that. "I didn't exactly prescribe it, Luke. Her son said he thought it was supposed to give people their energy back, so I told him to go ahead and give it. Lord knows it won't hurt Mrs. Adams, and it'll probably make that grown son of hers feel like he's doing something."

Another time Luke was obviously questioning what Pa had done. I thought he had a lot of nerve, but Pa just explained it to him real nice.

"There ain't a thing wrong with Miss Nelly. Can't be. All you did was hold her hand and listen to her talk."

"I took her temperature, too," Pa reminded him.

"Yeah, you did. Why?"

"So she'd feel like I was doing something. You're right. There's nothing wrong with her except she's lonely, she needs someone to pay attention to her. That's an important part of taking care of people, Luke. You have to take all of their lives into account, whether they're happy or worried or lonely or angry. It affects their health."

When Pa wasn't busy with patients, he pretty much holed up in his study, reading and writing. I guess he was working on some big project, but I didn't know what. I knew that Pa loved me, never doubted it for a minute, but for the time he had quite unconsciously shut me out of his life and that hurt. We had little real contact, and I missed Pa almost as much as I missed Mama.

Oh, sometimes he did try to talk to me, asking about my cooking or how did I spend my days or what had I read lately. I didn't have the heart to tell him I didn't have time to read, and I thought he should have already known how I spent my days. Once in a while, he still talked to me about patients and other things.

One night, he surprised me by saying "I talked with Mayor Clintlock today. He's still determined to raise that renegade army."

"You don't think he should, do you?"

"No, I don't. Senseless, that's what it is . . . just pure senseless, and innocent people will be involved . . . hurt, even killed." He stared off in space, lost in his own thoughts, and I went on with my mending, until Pa spoke again. "You know, Julie, so much of what happens to us is senseless . . ."

My heart jumped. He'd called me by Mama's name, and all the time I thought he was talking to me! "Pa . . ."

"What? Oh, sorry, Theo. Got lost in my own thoughts there for a moment. What were you saying?"

"Nothing, Pa. You were talking about Mayor Clintlock." **43**

"Yes, of course. For some reason, though I began to think about your mother again. I wish she could know . . ."

"Know what?"

"How much I miss her."

"I know you do, Pa."

I never told him how he hurt my feelings that night.

Luke was gone a lot of the time, too, though it puzzled me some to know where he went when he wasn't with Pa. Part of the time, I knew, he went out to his farm patch because he brought onions and greens and talked of carrots and squash and corn to come. I heard him tell Pa he'd been tending the crop real good, pests weren't too bad, and he expected a good amount of vegetables for us.

One time he picked a bunch of poke salad and handed it to me, saying, "I don't suppose you know how to cook this."

I did. Nan had been so scared of someone poisoning himself by not cooking poke the right way that she'd repeated over and over that you had to boil it twice and be sure to pour off all the first boiling water.

But several other times I had to accept cooking lessons from Luke, which galled me. He went hunting and, to my chagrin, proved to be a pretty good shot. He'd bring rabbit and squirrel, both of which he had to teach me to cook and neither of which I ever learned to like much. He tried for wild turkey but without any luck, even though he used his pa's trick of putting a leaf between his teeth to imitate their call. I laughed when he tried to show me.

Anyway, when the geese flew back north, Luke bagged a fat, young one and we feasted. That was the day he gave me a long lesson in picking shot out of a bird, and I crunched my teeth down on a bit of it anyway. Luke laughed that time.

But there were times, especially in the evening, that I had no idea where Luke went. He'd just disappear without a word to anyone, and hours later he'd come back, still without explanation. I asked once.

"Where've you been?"

"Oh, you know. Into town."

"At this hour? Luke Widman."

"You keepin' track of me?" He said it with a grin, but the question was serious.

A few days after Mr. Clintlock's visit, I found out where Luke had been going.

Mr. Jones had come for Pa to check his hand and take out some of the stitches. Luke was gone somewhere, so I was in the room with them because Pa said he might want my help to hand him things. That's how I came to learn about Luke's evening trips.

"That young Widman," Jones said conversationally, as Pa pried and snipped, "he sure is a real chip off the old block."

"That so?" Pa asked absently.

"Why, he sure is. Just like his pa. He comes to all those night meetings Clintlock calls and just sits and listens. That boy's ready to do his part when the time comes."

Now Pa was silent, but I knew he was listening carefully. Mr. Jones never noticed the silence and went right on with his monologue.

"Charles Widman, Luke's pa, he was a great one for defending his rights. I'm kind of surprised he left, being as how he was one of the first to talk about a local army for protection. Strange what grief will do to a man, ain't it? He just up and rode away."

Grimly, Pa echoed him. "Yes, it's strange what grief will do."

"Don't see you at those meetings, Doc. You just sendin' the boy as your representative?"

"I am not sending Luke at all," Pa said quietly, "and I am not there because I think the idea of a local militia is sheer folly."

45

Mr. Jones looked surprised, almost shocked, but he said nothing more and Pa continued his work in silence. I was so uncomfortable I could hardly wait to be out of the room, and I said a fervent thank-you when Pa said he didn't think he'd need me anymore.

"Bye, Mr. Jones. Hope your hand is okay."

"Well, now, thank you, missy. That's right kind of you. You tell that boy I'll look for him this evening."

"Run along, Theo," Pa said, his voice showing ever so slight a bit of irritation. Then he turned to Mr. Jones, and as I left I heard him say in a business-like tone, "There now, sir. That should not give you any more trouble. I recommend stretching and flexing your hand to limber it up as much as possible."

Pa and Luke had another talk that evening, once again closeted in Pa's study where I could not hear. I'd have given almost anything to know what went on between them, but the only clue I had was that Luke stayed home that evening. At least, he started to, until I made him mad.

He came up behind me while I sat on the edge of the dog-trot, as I did almost every night. Lots of times, Luke came and talked to me. Sometimes we bickered, and sometimes we talked about Canton or school or even what our futures held. But tonight, Luke was silent.

Finally, I asked timidly, "Pa mad at you?"

"Theo, your pa doesn't get angry." There was a long pause. "But we disagreed about something."

"I know. But, Luke, think how he feels about men taking the law into their own hands. You know he thinks that army is the most foolish thing ever."

"That may be, but my pa thought it was something we needed."

"Why?"

"Pa always said a man has to look out for himself first, and that you can't let the government push you around."

"Who's pushing you around, though?"

Luke hesitated a minute. "Well, you know . . . I mean, there's that trouble with the Klan, and there's always the chance Sheridan might send his occupation troops up here . . . we have to be ready."

"Is that what your pa told you?"

"Yeah."

"Luke, if he felt that strongly about it, why didn't he stay here to be part of that so-called army."

Even in the dark, I could almost see Luke's anger rise. Standing up suddenly, he muttered, "I knew you wouldn't understand, Theo," and walked deliberately away from the house.

He hadn't come back by the time I fell asleep, and I worried that Pa would be upset. Strangely enough, I also worried that Luke was mad at me again. This time, for once, I hadn't meant to make him angry. I just asked what I thought was a fair question.

Next morning, Luke appeared for breakfast, all silent and tired looking.

"Morning," he mumbled.

Pa came in just after that, nodded briefly at both of us, and sat at the table without a word. It was an uncomfortable meal, with no conversation beyond "Pass the salt" and "Thank you." I noticed that Luke kept looking around the room, anywhere

47

but at Pa, and Pa looked grim every time his glance fell on Luke.

As soon as he finished eating, Pa announced he had to make a house call and got up to leave. He looked at Luke, and Luke looked down at his plate, even though I knew he wanted badly to ask to go with Pa. After a minute, Pa just walked out of the room, and Luke went on eating.

Things went on that way in our house for several days. Pa and Luke weren't angry, but they weren't happy with each other either. And I was caught in the middle, feeling sorry for both of them and for myself. I was afraid to ask either one what had happened that night, but I kind of suspected that Pa had not forbidden Luke to go to the meeting. That wouldn't have been his way, because Pa generally expected people to make their own decisions and take the consequences. But he probably told Luke he would be mightily disappointed in him if he did go. And that, I supposed, was why Luke hung around instead of taking right off to town. He was torn between doing what he wanted and thought he ought to do for his pa's sake, and keeping the respect of my pa, which was awful important to him. I didn't know but what he would have stayed home altogether if I hadn't made that dumb remark about his pa and how he should never have left. But it was too late for second thoughts. Luke had gone, and he had disappointed Pa, and we all knew it.

4

NOT MUCH LATER, on a warm summer day, Luke and I forgot our anger and pride, and he and Pa swallowed their difficulties. We were all thrown together by a tragedy.

I was sitting out in the yard trying to forget the chores I hadn't done yet, while Pa was closeted in his study, doing whatever he did in there all the time. Luke came down the road at a terrible speed. I was about to say something smart about what was his rush or were his coattails on fire when I saw the color of his face. It was grey, almost white, and his eyes were wide with horror.

Spotting me, he shouted in a strained, unreal voice, "They lynched him, Theo! They hung him."

My first reaction was disbelief, like Luke had had a nightmare or something. I knew by his face that he wasn't joking, yet what he was saying was impossible. I couldn't figure out what to do or say next, but I didn't have to. Pa came to the edge of the dogtrot.

"They hung who, Luke?" He asked it in a quiet, almost everyday voice, and it calmed Luke down some, but he was still babbling when he answered.

"Web Turner, that's who! They just took him out by his own tank, and hung him from a tree."

Web Turner! My mind searched in corners until I remembered who Web Turner was. The old man who owned the tank where Luke took me fishing, the one who Luke said liked to be left alone all the time. But even as I figured out who Luke was talking about, I realized he was serious, dead serious. Someone had been hanged . . . and not just anyone, but someone Luke knew.

"Why would anyone hang him? And who did it?" My questions blurted out, propelled by my own confusion.

"Just a minute, Theo. Luke needs to collect himself." That was Pa, calm even at a time like this. He turned to Luke and spoke gently. "Calm down, now, son, and when you're ready, you tell me about it. Here, have a cold drink." Pa walked over to the pump and drew a dipperful of water for Luke.

"Thank you, sir." Luke wiped one grimy sleeve across his forehead and gulped the water. It proved to be a mistake, for he stood there just a moment, then bolted around the corner of the house. After a minute, we could hear the clear sound of Luke throwing up.

Pa and I just stood there and looked at each other. Pa had the most grim look I'd ever seen. It reminded me some of the way he used to look after he'd come home from The War. But he never spoke a word.

Luke came back, head hanging and looking now more green than grey but not much better. He mumbled an apology, but Pa reached out and put an arm around his shoulders.

"It's all right, son. You've had one of the worst shocks a man can have. Death by violence, senseless violence, is an awful, incomprehensible thing."

I thought maybe Pa should have left out incomprehensible. I wasn't sure what it meant, and I knew Luke wouldn't know. But Pa went right on in his comforting tone of voice.

"Now, come in and sit down and we'll talk about it. Theo, bring a cold cloth for Luke's face, please."

I got a cloth and pretty soon we were all three settled in the cool and dark comfort of Pa's study.

"Did you see Web Turner, son?"

"Yes," Luke whispered. "I . . . I was gonna catch some fish for dinner—now that Theo knows how to fry them." He managed a slight grin in my direction. "So, I went out to the tank. And there he was, across the water, hanging from one of them big trees right at the edge."

"Could you see him clearly?"

"No, but I could tell it was him. I know his old red plaid shirt and those coveralls he always wears. Weren't nobody else."

"I'm sure you're right, Luke, but I'm grateful you were spared the sight of a hanged man. It's . . . it's horrible." Pa lost his calming manner for a moment in a huge shudder. I suppose sometime he'd seen a hanged man, but I didn't know.

Luke was getting more talkative now. "I thought maybe I should go over and do something . . . you know, cut him down . . . but I . . . well, truth is, I was scared."

"That was sensible of you, Luke. Cutting the poor fellow down is a job for men anyway. I don't suppose you've told anyone else about this . . . this atrocity?"

I sighed. Another of Pa's big words.

Luke said he hadn't told anybody, and Pa said as soon as Luke felt up to it, they'd best go to town and notify Sheriff Browder.

I opened my mouth to protest, and Pa stopped me before I could speak. "You come too, Theo. I don't imagine you much feel like staying here alone."

"No, I don't." The whole world seemed spooky to me, and I wouldn't have been left alone for anything.

Luke really didn't feel like going to town yet, so we just sat and talked.

"Tell me what you know about Web Turner," Pa suggested.

"He was a loner, most I know," said Luke. "Folks used to say he was a . . . what did they call them people against slavery?"

"Abolitionist?"

"Yeah, that's it. Used to be rumors around that he hid runaway slaves, and that's why he never let anybody on his place." He paused a little. "I never did believe that. He was just an old man who wanted to be left alone."

"You knew him?"

"About as well as anyone did, I guess." Luke got that far-away look in his eyes, and I felt real sorry for him. It's bad enough to hear that a stranger's been lynched, but it's a whole different story to think of anything like that happening to a real person you've known.

"He used to let me fish out there . . . taught me a little about fishing, too. Never went out of his way to be friendly when he saw me, but he . . . well, he tolerated me. That's more than he did for most people."

Pa nodded as if he were piecing it together in his mind. "Did he have any other friends?"

"Nope." Luke seemed very positive about that. "When he had to go to town, he just went about his business and didn't talk to nobody. Folks thought he was kind of touched in the head, but I don't think so."

My skin crawled. Web Turner had been just a name to me, but now that he was dead, he was taking on form and becoming a real personality. I was glad when Pa asked Luke if he didn't think we should go to the sheriff's office now.

We passed Edgeworth's store and the school and even saw Arley Clintlock in the street and nodded to him, but we kept on directly heading for the courthouse and Sheriff Browder. I looked at Mayor Clintlock and couldn't help thinking to myself, "Wait till he hears!" It was all I could do to keep from running over and spilling all about the lynching. Knowing something others don't, even if it's as horrible as a lynching, is a real temptation. It makes you feel kind of powerful, and that's wrong.

Sheriff Browder didn't believe us at first. "Nobody's ever been lynched in this county . . . 'cept one murderer about ten years ago . . . the kid must have seen something else and let his imagination run away with him." The sheriff leaned back in his chair, his fat belly sticking out, and spat accurately into the spittoon.

"I saw him hanging there." Luke said it in a quiet but determined tone of voice.

"Sheriff, I know it's hard to believe, but I'm pretty sure about Luke's accuracy. I think we'd better check."

"You gonna go with me?"

Pa looked resigned. "Yes, I'll go. Theo, you and Luke wait here."

The sheriff found a horse for Pa, but he didn't take it seriously enough to take a horse out there for Web Turner's body. They rode off and left us sitting there kind of dreading their return.

"Will they bring it, uh, him with them?" I asked.

"Don't know, Theo. Oh, Theo, if you'd seen . . . it was . . . well, I just can't imagine anything so horrible."

The horror of it drew us together, and we sat in silence for a long time. One man wandered into the office, a man I didn't know, but he was obviously a farmer, dressed in coveralls with dirty hands that he waved in the air.

"Sheriff gone?" he demanded.

"Yeah," Luke muttered. "Ought to be back soon."

"Tell him I'm gonna shoot Mrs. Johnson's milk cow if it wanders on to my place again. Just wanted him to know. Makes it all legal." And he left as nonchalantly as he'd entered.

"Luke, why didn't you tell him where they've gone?"

"Wasn't any of his business."

"No, but he ought to know Sheriff Browder will have more important things on his mind than a wandering milk cow."

"He'll find out."

Luke was right. The whole town found out shortly after Pa and the sheriff came back. They didn't bring the body— Sheriff Browder rounded up a deputy and sent him out with a horse to fetch it to Mr. Jones, the butcher who also served as undertaker when the need arose. But they brought back something almost more important than the body—a note.

Sheriff Browder was holding it in his hand, creasing it over and over in a nervous gesture, as they walked back in. "Did you know about this, son?" He waved it at Luke.

"What about it?" Luke asked, clearly letting his ignorance show.

"Note. Left by the Klan."

Luke and I both gasped. We'd heard all about the Klan cell down south, but like Mayor Clintlock and Pa said, the closest

54

they'd ever come to Canton was Tyler. There'd never been any trouble near us, and we thought of the dreaded and horrible Klan as something far away. It wasn't possible that it had reached its long arm into our county.

I knew Pa was more upset than ever. The Klan stood for all the things he opposed . . . violence, lack of reason. He'd talked to both of us about it one night after Mayor Clintlock had brought the subject up. Pa said it was the worst way ever to deal with violence and said that anyone who hid behind a sheet was a coward. Besides, he told us, the big worry was that people like the Klan would be undisciplined and as likely to hang an innocent man as a guilty one. Pa believed in the justice system of our country, and he said that was how any unruly citizens, black or white, should be dealt with. Now, his worst fears seemed to have come true. The Klan had lynched the wrong man for sure.

I got up my nerve to speak. "What does the note say?"

"Says here," said the Sheriff, unfolding the now-tattered note and reading in the careful, uncertain manner of one only partially educated, "Let this be a warning to all others—the Klan will not be blocked or crossed."

"What do you suppose that means, Sheriff?" Pa asked.

"I suppose they believe all those rumors about old Turner having hid runaways . . . could be true but that ain't good reason to hang a man."

"It is to the Klan," Pa said bitterly. "They've already gone beyond their original purpose, which was just to bring order where Sheridan's troops weren't enforcing the law. Now they're trying to force everyone to think their way."

"But why Web Turner?" Luke asked, as though maybe he could reverse it all if there was no good reason.

"Told ya," the sheriff said, "they thought he was a friend of the blacks."

"Killing him," Pa went on, "would frighten anybody else who might think like this poor Turner fellow . . . and it enlarges the area where people live in fear of the Klan. Gives them more power."

It was all confusing to me. I still couldn't see why they'd killed that poor old man.

55

"Sheriff," Pa said, "if you need a doctor on your posse, I am honor bound to go."

That was a big thing for Pa to do, feeling as he did about violence. But if he was going to support law and order, he had to make that offer. I understood thoroughly that Pa was caught between a rock and a hard place, and I hurt for him.

"I'll go too," Luke said determinedly.

I knew what was next. I was to be sent home while the men did their business. It just wasn't fair. But the Sheriff surprised all of us.

"Hold on, now, just a minute. Who said anything about a posse?"

"What else can you do?" Pa asked.

"Notify government headquarters down south," the sheriff said, stroking his fat chin as though thinking. "I doubt you'll find enough men in this town who want to tangle with the Klan."

He was wrong. By now, the town knew what had happened, since the deputy who went to fetch Web Turner's body had a loose tongue and hadn't fought off the temptation to tell the way I had. There were knots of men milling around the courthouse when we went outside.

Pa stopped to talk to a group, and I kind of wandered around, listening to the conversations. One or two men were afraid of the Klan but most were ready to fight.

"Ain't gonna get me to ride against them," said one man, hitching up the strap on his overalls.

"But you can't just let them get away with this!" exclaimed the man next to him. He, too, wore stained and dirty work clothes, but he had an intense look on his face and his fists were clenched.

"Hell I can't! If it means my skin, I can," was the reply.

I heard another protest to the man next to him about law and order, and the man kind of sighed. "You're right, you sure are. But you gonna be the one to tell my wife and kids the Klan got me too?"

"No," the first man said, "I'm gonna be the one ridin' with you."

But there was another thread of conversation that dominated as these men stood shuffling dirt in work-worn boots and wiping grimy hands on tattered overalls. They were indignant that their county had been invaded.

"Van Zandt County never had no trouble like that . . . why'd they come over here to do their dirty work?"

"Yeah. We're getting along pretty peaceful here. Down to San Augustine and thereabouts, that's where they're having trouble. Bet we haven't had three outside niggers ride through here since the war . . . and none of them stayed."

"I hear," said someone else, "some those free blacks down there are terrified, desperate to get out of the Klan's reach. Bet they thought ol' Turner was still helping blacks escape— only this time escaping from the Klan instead of some owner with bloodhounds."

"We ought to show them they can't come riding up here whenever they feel like lynching somebody . . . this here is the Free State of Van Zandt."

Pa shook his head in despair, and I knew what he was thinking. Some of the men were ready to ride in a posse for all the wrong reasons. Not because a man had been killed, but because their territory had been invaded. They wanted revenge, not law and order. Such a posse would amount to fighting violence with violence, and Pa could see clearly that it would only make things worse.

In the end, there was no posse. Not because the men weren't willing but because the sheriff refused to organize one. I really think he was afraid, but the reason he gave was that the Klan would have already ridden out of his jurisdiction, and it was a matter for Sheridan's occupation government. He sent word right away, he said, but everyone knew that it would be too late by the time the army moved. Besides, the army hadn't done much about the Klan so far. Why would they now?

I asked Pa, though, if notifying the government wasn't right and what he would have done.

"Yes, Theo, but a posse might have caught those men and held them for the authorities. This way, they'll never be found."

Luke had been quiet through all this, and he still looked thoughtful as he finally spoke. "You wouldn't have them lynched?"

"Absolutely not," Pa said. "That makes it an eye for an eye. You would be no better than they were."

"But you would chase them?" Luke persisted.

"Yes, I would have, Luke, but it's the sheriff's responsibility. I can't take the law into my own hands any more than the Klan can."

"But you would see them punished." It was a statement, not a question, and Luke looked satisfied as he said it.

Ours was a silent and subdued house that evening. Late at night, I sat outside trying to understand all that had happened. Pa was writing furiously at his desk, recording the day's events I guess. Luke had gone to sleep, so he said, but I swore I heard him sobbing into his pillow, ever so quietly so no one would know, but still sobbing.

The lynching dominated everything for days, and people talked of little else.

"Horrible, just horrible," Mrs. Edgeworth said when I

went in for staples. "Why that Mr. Turner was always a nice, polite man when he came in here. Never said a cross word to anyone. I considered I knew him well."

I nodded and agreed with her, but privately I was thinking how funny it is that people get to know a man real well after he's dead when in real life they didn't know him much at all.

"How's that poor boy out at your house, Theo? He's had one grief after another, hasn't he? First his ma, then his pa leaving, now he has to be the one to find that horrible thing the other day."

"Luke's getting on fine," I said.

And, in truth, Luke was getting on fine, but he'd changed. For one thing, he'd lost some of that cocky sureness I'd resented before. And ever since the lynching, he'd stayed close to home, as though he were afraid he'd find another body if he went fishing. And he and I had extended our truce. We avoided the areas of real disagreement between us—like Pa and jealousy—and he didn't tease me about my cooking or anything. He really tried to help me. "Here, Theo, let me sweep" or "Theo, I'll carry that wash." To my surprise, I desperately missed the jokes and teasing. The changed Luke made me so nervous that I talked to Pa about him.

"Luke will be all right," he assured me. "He's had a major shock, the kind some men are spared all their lives. In time, he'll be back to what you call the old Luke . . . but, Theo, this will live with him all his life."

I nodded solemnly.

They buried Web Turner in a quiet ceremony three days after the lynching. No relatives had been turned up, and the county paid burial expenses, but there was a large crowd at the graveside services where Brother Anderson preached about the sin of taking another life. Maybe all those people came to show their anger at what had happened, and maybe some just came because people always want to be on the edges of a tragedy. But what was sad was that no one, except Luke, came because they'd known Web Turner.

I was glad Brother Anderson said in his prayer, "Oh, Lord, forgive those who put their own safety above right, and help them to find the way to follow your teachings." I glanced at the Sheriff, but I don't think he ever understood what Brother Anderson meant.

Pa had another visit from Mayor Clintlock a day or so later, and this time he didn't even bother to close the door. Luke and I both listened.

"Just came to tell you, Doc, that I'm getting lots of support for a Van Zandt Army after this, ahem, tragedy of . . ." His voice trailed off, and I suspected he couldn't remember Web Turner's name.

Pa supplied it for him.

"Yes, that's it, Web Turner. Fine fellow. But I wanted to ask you again to serve us as physician. It's your duty."

"My duty to whom?" Pa asked.

"Why, your neighbors."

"My duty is to do what I believe right," Pa said, "and that means I will have nothing to do with this scheme. My duty is also to set an example for Theo and Luke, which further rules out my participation."

"Now, Doc," Mr. Clintlock tried to be soothing, "we ain't gonna march off and start something. We're just gonna spread the word that we've armed ourselves. Why, that Klan will stay clean away from here. They're cowards, every last one of them."

"I surely agree with you that the Klansmen are cowards," Pa told him, "but I cannot agree to fight them by their own methods. It is now a matter for the authorities."

"Authorities, bah!" Clintlock said. "We're the authority around here. It's our county, not Sheridan's, not the U.S. government's. Our land belongs to us . . . we got rights."

5

THE LYNCHING did not fade quickly nor easily from our minds. It was nothing we talked about, but Luke and I both carried that horrible incident around with us for a long time.

The army did not fade from my mind, either, and Luke and I did talk about that. I knew very well how strongly Pa was opposed to violence and how right he was about the dangers of men taking justice into their own hands. And I thought the idea of a tiny, local army was almost funny. What kind of battles did they expect to win, I wondered? But a part of my mind believed, with Arley Clintlock, that the idea of an army would keep the Klan away from us, and I was most anxious never ever to have the Ku Klux Klan come back to Van Zandt County. As it turned out, I didn't get my wish, but I didn't know that the day Luke and I talked about the army.

"Luke, did you hear any more about Arley Clintlock's silly old army?" Now why I said it that way, I don't know. The word silly was bound to bring a reaction from Luke. Sometimes, I just seemed to be contrary on purpose when it came to Luke.

"It ain't silly, Theo. If you understood things . . ."

"I understand it all right. It's wrong, just like Pa said."

"Your Pa doesn't understand either. That army would be a good thing for this county, keep us safe, even give us more of a voice with the government."

I giggled. "A voice that would be a cry for help when the government took over your army," I laughed. "How can one little county fight off the U.S. government?"

"Oh, Theo, for pity's sake. Nobody's gonna fight the government. We're just going to protect our rights, and show that we can't be walked over." Luke had been listening to the mayor. His words sounded more like Arley Clintlock than Luke Widman.

"Who's we?" I asked.

He looked startled. "Why, the men of Van Zandt County, of course."

I bit my tongue to keep from laughing again, this time at his including himself with the men. Instead, I said something that sounded like Pa, only coming from me it was pompous.

"One thing leads to another. That army will just bring trouble."

"Oh, stop being so smart."

"Well, anyway, is there an army? Have they marched or whatever it is armies do to practice?"

He looked purely disgusted. "No, they haven't. And I wouldn't tell you if they had." With that he walked deliberately away.

The days passed slowly as summer came upon us in its full strength. The air was hot and heavy, and often by mid-day, I wanted to do no more than sit in a chair and read. Evenings, it was sticky and near impossible to sleep. My temper grew shorter and shorter as we suffered through one hot spell after another, and it was an effort to wash clothes or even sweep the floor. Some days it seemed like we lived on melons. There'd been a good crop to the east of us, and some of the farmers sold their melons off carts by the courthouse in town. They were cheap and good, and we ate our fill while the season lasted. Luke had raised a good vegetable crop on his pa's land, and we had lots of vegetables too—squash and kale, which I didn't like much, and peas and beans. Many nights we had greens and cornbread and never missed the meat.

It was one of those hot summer days that something happened to change our lives. I remembered it afterwards as the day of the chickens. Luke had been insisting for a long time that we needed chickens, and I agreed. We rarely had eggs, costly as they were, and I supposed I could learn to pluck an occasional chicken if Luke would be the one to wring its neck. Pa's gentlemanly instincts rebelled at the thought of chickens running loose in his yard. I know to his mind that was how poor folk lived. But, finally, he agreed we could get a rooster and five hens if Luke would be responsible for them. This meant Luke had to make a chicken house out of an old shed behind our cabin and fence around it so the chickens could be out but wouldn't be loose. Luke agreed to set right to work repairing the shed, and Pa gave him money for chicken wire. Luke did a right smart job of fencing. When he was all through, he even used some scrap lumber he found to build crates to bring the chickens home in. Then he borrowed a wheelbarrow from somewhere—Luke was amazing at being able to borrow whatever was needed at just the right moment—and we were ready for chickens. He'd already made arrangements with Mr. Jones to get them, of course.

We set out for the butcher shop early that morning while it was still cool. We were in fairly high spirits and, for once, both of us were on the same side of a project, so we were getting along well.

"What you gonna name them hens, Theo?"

"Me? I thought they were your chickens."

"Yeah, but I'll only name the rooster. You can do the others."

"Oh, I see. I get to name the insignificant females but you'll choose the important name."

"That's right. Gonna call the rooster Lochinvar."

"Lochinvar? What for?"

"He was some man . . . from Scotland, I think . . . who had a real way with the ladies. And this rooster's gonna be the same."

"Oh, you think so. I'll call the hens Esmerelda and Matilda and . . . let's see, maybe Amelia May after my best friend in Mississippi."

"Theo! Those are horrible names! Can't you pick something simple, like . . . well, why not call one Theo?"

I gave him a good kick, then ran quickly before he could drop the wheelbarrow in the dusty road and catch me. He did drop it long enough to pick up a handful of dry dust and fling it in my direction, but, laughing at his miss, I ran beyond his reach.

Mr. Clintlock was standing leaning against the brick doorway of his bank, looking one way and another up and down the street. We smiled hello but he barely acknowledged us. Mrs. Edgeworth, busily rearranging the goods in her window, gave us a much more cheerful wave, and we both waved back, which almost caused Luke to drop the wheelbarrow on his toe. I laughed again and was still grinning when we reached the butcher shop.

"We've come for Luke's chickens, Mr. Jones."

"Luke's chickens, huh?" He wiped his hands on the filthy dirty apron he was wearing, and I tried not to figure too hard on what spots were what. The whole butcher shop was dirty, with counters that needed dusting, bloodstains on the floor from his cutting up of meat, and a spotted scale on which he weighed your purchases. I was glad we didn't buy much from Mr. Jones.

"You got the crates, boy?"

"Yes, sir." I knew Luke hated to be called "boy," but he was polite and said nothing.

"Come on out back, and I'll let you pick your hens."

Mr. Jones kept a large chickenhouse behind his shop, but I'd been out there once before and had no wish to go with them. It smelled even worse than the heavy odor of the butcher shop, if that was possible. I decided to wait out in the street.

The butcher shop had a wooden sidewalk in front of it, and a small roof over that supported by rough cut poles. I leaned against one of the poles and stared up at the sky. There were clouds but not the kind that would bring rain, and I was marveling at this part of the country where for a while we had so much rain, too much, and now we would have given our eye teeth for a cooling storm.

Still, it was a pretty day, with just a hint of breeze, and I was standing in the midst of Canton where I could watch the town's comings and goings rather than being at home washing clothes, so I was feeling pretty good about things. At first, when I heard the horses behind me, I hardly paid any attention. But it dawned on me that there were far too many horses coming far too fast. Several men who'd been lounging against the courthouse bolted for a nearby building, and Old Man Brewster, who couldn't move fast if he had to, stood rooted to the spot staring in horror at what was approaching him.

The hairs on the back of my neck prickled, and I turned just as the horses drew even with me. At first, I thought I couldn't make my eyes focus. Everything was white and shapeless. Then it came to me like a great sinking feeling. That was the awful, the dreaded Klan riding right into Canton—and riding like they meant business. For one terrible moment, I just stood there, hypnotized by the sight of those men draped in white. Even their faces were covered with white masks, and they wore tall, pointed white hats.

"Girlie! Psst!" Mr. Jones called softly from the back of his shop. "Come in here, but come slow."

I obeyed, somehow quieting the urge to jump and run. In the shadows in the back of the butcher shop, Mr. Jones and Luke stood huddled together whispering. When I ap-

proached, they stopped talking to each other and turned to me.

"See how many of them there are, Theo?"

"No. Lots."

"I'd say ten, maybe twelve," Mr. Jones said. "Can you do this, boy?"

Luke looked solemn, but he nodded. "Theo, you've got to help. I'm . . ."

Before he could finish, shots filled the air and the three of us froze.

It seemed like forever that we stood there motionless, but it must not have been long before Mr. Jones broke the silence, by whispering, "Probably just warning shots. Boy, can you creep up there and see?"

"Sure." Luke crawled on hands and knees to the door, then seeming to stop and hold his breath, he peeked ever so carefully around the edge, keeping low where they might not expect to see a head. After a minute, he stood up and walked back to us, bold as you please.

"They're riding in circles around the courthouse, must have fired those shots in the air. But they ain't paying no attention to anyone around."

"Old Man . . . I mean, Mr. Brewster . . . is he . . . ?"

"He's walking down the street away from them. Seems okay."

"Oh." I could still see the frightened look on that man's face. Of course, who wouldn't be frightened, after what they had done to Web Turner?

"Can't Sheriff Browder make them leave?" I realized as I asked that it was a dumb question.

Luke laughed, but Mr. Jones looked disgusted. "Sheriff? He's probably hiding behind his desk right now. Klan terrifies him. We'll have to handle this . . . and we need Luke."

A flash of terror swept through me. What was Luke going to do? I stared at both of them, waiting for an explanation.

Luke hitched at his overalls and motioned for me to follow him out the back. "You got to take this wheelbarrow full of chickens home, Theo . . . I'll be along right soon. But you go on."

"Me? Take those chickens? Luke!" I forgot my terror in indignation. I wasn't going to push a wheelbarrow full of chickens.

"Theo, hush. It's gotta be."

"Luke, I'm scared."

"Who's gonna bother a dumb old girl with a wheelbarrow full of chickens?"

"Luke Widman, wait 'til I tell Pa."

That was the first thing I said that really got his attention.

"Theo, please, it's important. Don't tell. I'll . . . I'll, oh heck. I'll do something special for you. But don't tell. He wouldn't understand and . . . well, there's just something I got to do."

"Luke, you're babbling. What are you going to do?"

"Just go warn people, Theo. We got this all figured out."

Mr. Jones nodded. "You know where to go, boy?"

Luke said he did and was out the back of the shop before I could say any more to him. Reluctantly, I picked up the handles of the wheelbarrow.

"Go this back way 'til you're well away from the courthouse," Mr. Jones said.

The wheelbarrow was heavy and awkward, bouncing on rocks and sometimes throwing dust back at me. The chickens scolded and obviously didn't like the ride any better than I did. And the day had gotten hotter, so that my face felt sweaty and hot, and my hair stuck to my forehead. I walked along thinking of exquisite ways of getting back at Luke Widman. A snake in his bed would be too good for him. But at the same time, I was worried about him . . . and curious about what was all worked out in advance. It was beginning to sound to me like Luke was not just a listener at the meetings in The Clancey Inn—he was a real part of that army. And that meant more trouble between Pa and Luke.

"Theo, why are you bringing those chickens?" Pa was standing on the dogtrot when I came home, hands in the pockets of that same dark suit he always wore. He'd apparently been pacing back and forth which is what he did a lot when he was especially worried. "Where's Luke? I heard shots from the center of town."

"The Klan rode in."

"The Klan? Theo, you must be mistaken."

"No, I'm not!" I was hot and indignant enough to be sharp-tongued even with my father. "How could I mistake those white outfits? There were ten or twelve of them, at least that's what Mr. Jones said."

"Mr. Jones? Did you see them yourself?"

"Could have reached out and touched one if I'd have wanted."

Pa almost smiled. "Well, I'm glad you didn't want. Where's Luke?"

It was my moment of truth. Was I going to tattle? When it came right down to it, I couldn't tell on Luke, mad as I was at him. "He, uh, stayed to help Mr. Jones with something. He'll be home directly."

Pa didn't say a word, just turned and went into his office. Whereas some men might have taken right off to see the trouble or to help defend their hometown, that wasn't Pa's way. It wasn't that he was afraid for himself, though I suspect he was worried some about Luke. But it was his feelings about violence that kept him home in his study. He could do no good at this moment, and he knew it, much better than either Luke or I understood.

Violence finally did reach out to our cabin to touch us but not until late in the day. I spent an uneasy, long day, waiting for Luke, listening for noise from the courthouse, and turning to stone in terror when I heard shots late in the afternoon. Pa was home all day, with not one patient needing him. I suppose they were all afraid to stick their heads out their doors and would not have come in an emergency. When I heard the shooting, I was out in the back looking at Luke's chickens, wishing that Lochinvar and his ladies could distract me from my worry about Luke. I bolted for Pa's study at the sound of gunfire.

"Pa! Pa, did you hear that?"

"The shots? Yes, Theo, I heard them."

"Is it . . . do you think . . . I mean, where's Luke?"

"I suspect he's fine, just fine," Pa said reassuringly. I couldn't tell if he really believed that or was just saying it for me. But then he offered a very logical explanation, which I readily accepted. "Sounds to me like that's just shots in the air. Show-off stuff." The contempt in his voice was clear.

Much later, we found out that Pa was wrong. Those shots were aimed deliberately, and they hit someone. But it was a while before we knew that, and Luke was safely home by then.

He came up to the cabin from the opposite direction, walking slowly and looking awful, like he was more tired than he'd ever been. Dirt and sweat were streaked across his face, and he'd gotten so hot he'd taken off his shirt and stuffed it in his back pocket. Somehow, the sight of him shirtless under his coveralls made me think of the extra layer of clothing the Klansmen wore—that silly sheet—and I hoped they were suffering heat prostration, whatever that is. I even giggled at the thought, which temporarily enraged Luke.

"Think I look funny, huh? Fine lot you know about it." As his parting insult, he muttered a scornful, "Girls!" under his breath as he walked by me.

"Luke, I wasn't laughing at you. I really wasn't."

He looked doubtful, so I made amends by bringing him a dipper of water. He drank it slowly, and I tried to explain about the sheets and how hot I thought those awful men must be.

"It ain't funny, Theo. Nothing about those men is funny." His voice was weary, but then he added with a touch of steel determination, "But we're gonna show 'em. We really are."

"Who's we?" I asked, awe-struck. Was there to be an outright fight?

"Can't tell you now. Just you wait."

Pa came out of his study, looked Luke over for a long minute, and then went and put an arm around his shoulders. "Glad you're back, son. I worried about you, and I'd rather think you weren't mixed up in the foolishness that's going on in town."

Luke stubbed a toe at the ground and avoided looking Pa in the eye. "I . . . I wasn't in town much of today. But, you know, sir, the men will have to defend Canton. It's . . . it's our home. That's what my pa always told me."

There he went, talking about his pa again. Fine thing, I thought, to be loyal to a man who just rode off and left, never sent word in all the three months or so he'd been gone.

"If you weren't in town, where were you?" Pa asked quietly, his arm still around Luke's shoulders.

"I . . . well, I went to . . ."

"To alarm the county?"

"Not exactly, but . . . yeah, that's the plan Mr. Jones and Mayor Clintlock worked out last week, just in case. Said it would be too obvious if any of them left town if there was trouble, but a boy could do it and not be noticed. I been walkin' most of the day."

"No wonder you're tired!" I gasped, feeling sorry for him that he'd had to walk all day but kind of proud that he'd done his share.

Pa didn't see it that way at all. "Just adding fuel to the fire, Luke. Those men will leave town . . . they've got nothing to gain by staying in Canton. Just showing off." There was the same tone of contempt I'd heard earlier. "I pray now they leave before there's a fight and people are killed."

Luke looked startled for a moment, as though the thought of death hadn't occurred to him. Pa took advantage of that moment.

"You're not playing a boy's game of war, Luke. The men you alarmed today will kill at the drop of a hat."

"They're only protecting . . ." Luke began, but his voice drifted away, and he stood lost in thought.

72

After a little bit, Pa asked Luke about the shots we'd heard but Luke hadn't even heard them, didn't know anything about them.

Darkness came late on long summer nights, but it was dark this night when we heard men approaching down the road. Though they spoke softly, it sounded like there was a whole bunch of them. I was ready to jump off the dogtrot and investigate, but Pa put a hand on my arm.

"Wait, Theo. Let me go."

He stepped out into the road and peered into the darkness. I hoped it wasn't the Klan because Pa stood in the light coming from the cabin, and the men were still in the dark. In a moment, though, I was reassured by several voices.

"Doc? Thank God you're here."

There was a kind of chorus of similar murmurs, and as the men neared, I could see there were about six of them. One man seemed unable to walk and was supported by two of his companions.

"What's the trouble, gentlemen?"

"Hanson here got shot in the ankle."

"Those shots I heard earlier in the afternoon?"

"Sure were. Those buzzards had us cornered though, and we couldn't get out of the bank to bring him 'til dark came."

"Get him inside. Let me look at it."

I knew what was coming and ran quick as I could to put an old sheet on the fainting couch. I didn't want this Mr. Hanson, a man I'd never met, bleeding all over our only good piece of furniture. Pa needed a table, I thought. Pa must have thought about it, too, for he was even quicker than me.

"Lay him here on the floor, gentlemen. I can work better there than on the couch. Theo, bring the light closer. Get me all the lamps you can."

I put the lamp down and knelt near Pa, stealing a look at the injured man's ankle. It was a mess of blood and torn pants, and I didn't look close enough to see more. Around me, I could feel the tension of the nervous, edgy men who stood there.

Pa muttered, "Buckshot," then turned to the men. "I'll need two of you to help. Rest will wait outside."

Hanson spoke for the first time, his eyes wide with fear. "Doc, sure hope you can help . . . I was in the war, and I know about . . . oh, hell, give me another swig." He reached a hand and one of the men produced a bottle. Hanson took a deep drink.

"Give him a drink as often as he wants it," Pa told the man, nodding at the others in dismissal. They shuffled out the door, murmuring among themselves, and I could hear them settle down on the creaking wood floor of the dogtrot. The man with the whisky bottle and the one other who had stayed both looked apprehensive.

"I'll need you to hold him down," Pa said. "Give the bottle to Luke, and he can give Mr. Hanson a drink whenever he needs it. I have no ether."

Hanson spoke again, this time desperate. "Doc, I got to tell you this. In that war, I saw it . . . you know, when they cut a man's leg off. Don't do it to me, don't do it to me!"

"Rest easy, Hanson. It looks to me like the shot shattered the bone, but I'll do my best to set it. Got to clean out the wound first, and that might take a while. You lie back and drink that whisky."

After telling me to mind the lamps, Pa knelt and began to cut away the pants leg, then probe gently with his instruments. I'd put a sheet on the floor next to him, and he put his instruments on one side and methodically began to pile up pieces of shot on the other. Trouble was, the shot had taken dirt and cloth into the man's leg with it, and it was painstaking, slow work to clean that ankle. I knew other doctors might have amputated—it would have been easier—and I was proud of Pa for working so hard on this man's leg.

Pa talked gently as he worked, reassuring Hanson as much as he could. "It's not too bad, Hanson. Think we can save it, but there's an awful risk of infection. You'll have to help me keep it clean."

Hanson nodded and reached for the bottle again. Luke helped him drink.

My back and legs ached from being on the floor, helping Pa when he needed something to mop up blood or reached for an instrument, and I knew Pa's back must be screaming in protest. But he never changed the pace of his slow, careful work. After what seemed hours, Pa spoke more firmly to his patient.

"The bone is shattered in one spot. I'm going to treat it like a break. Mean's I'll have to position it and there will be pain . . . probably pretty bad . . . but you must lie still." Pa emphasized the word "must," then turned to the other two men who'd been standing in the shadows. "Now is when I need you to hold him perfectly still."

Hanson took a long swallow from the bottle, then said thickly, "Okay, Doc, let's get it over with."

Even after what Pa said, I was unprepared for the loud cry of pain that came from Hanson when Pa positioned that bone. It was the only sound the man had made, and it both terrified and sickened me. I snuck a glance at Luke, and he, too, looked white. But he continued to hold the bottle. I remembered the time he'd watched Pa sew up Mr. Jones' hand, and I guessed Luke had really come a long ways in three months.

Pa had to cauterize parts of the wound where there was still blood oozing, and he sent me for the alcohol burner so he could heat the knife. I'd helped him one other time when he'd had to do this, and I wanted desperately to run from the room before the smell of burning flesh overcame me. But I gritted my teeth and stayed, eyeing Luke nervously to see how he'd do. Funny, I thought, just a little while ago I'd have been hoping Luke would bolt and run, disgrace himself in front of Pa and these men. Now, I was saying silent prayers for him to be all right until it was over.

Now Hanson groaned each time a new thrust of pain hit him, and Luke almost automatically gave him more of the whisky. I thought the man must be getting awfully drunk, and I noticed that when Pa wasn't actively probing or cauterizing, Hanson seemed to drift off into sleep. But each time Pa applied carbolic acid paste to clean the wound or took another stitch to close it, Hanson clutched his hands into a fist, his knuckles white, and uttered a small, pitiful sound.

Finally, Pa swathed the ankle in clean bandages I'd brought and it was over. We'd been in that stuffy office nearly three hours, and we were all stiff and sore when we finally stood up. I was sleepier than I'd been in a long time, but Luke looked alert, almost as if the whole thing had given him extra energy.

"Leave him right where he is, gentlemen," Pa said, stretching his arms high over his head to relieve the kinks in his back. "Theo, can you boil these gentlemen some coffee?"

"Yes, Pa." Coffee! What I wanted was sleep.

"I'll get the wood," Luke volunteered and was gone before I could blink.

Pa stood on the dogtrot and talked to the men, while I made the coffee. I could hear the conversation easily through the open door.

"It gonna be all right, Doc?"

"Can't tell. Infection is the big problem. There's the possibility, always the possibility, that I'll have to amputate."

A horrified murmur ran among the men. I guess each of them was worried about his friend but glad it was Hanson and not himself.

"But if you don't . . ."

"He'll never walk again like he did," Pa said with finality. "That leg will be short, that ankle stiff. That man will carry the Klan's mark the rest of his life." Pa had that same grim look he used to have when the men in Green City came back from The War.

"We'll get the bastards!" This announcement from one of the men was met with a chorus of agreement.

I came to the door in time to see Pa turn and walk into

his office, maybe to check on his patient and maybe to be away from the talk of revenge. In a minute or so, Luke followed him.

6

THE MEN ALL LEFT a little while later. I gave them hot coffee, and I guess they figured Pa wasn't going to come back out and talk any more, so they drifted away with mumbled thanks and praise for Pa.

"Your pa's a good doctor, Miss" and "Glad he understood things." I hadn't the nerve to tell them how little Pa sympathized with their attitude.

When the last one had gone, I knocked softly on Pa's door.

"Come in," he answered.

"The men have all left, Pa."

"Good, Theo. Luke and I were just discussing the evening's events. Weren't we, Luke?"

Luke nodded his head but said little, and I had the feeling perhaps Pa was discussing and Luke was mostly listening. Mr. Hanson still slept soundly on the floor, and I imagined all the whisky he'd had would mean he'd sleep through the night, which was good. When he awoke in the morning, he'd be in a lot of pain.

"Luke was telling me that it was an accident that Hanson was shot," Pa said, "and I was explaining that such accidents are the rule rather than the exception when men resort to violence." Pa sounded preachy.

"It was an accident," Luke protested. "Someone's gun went off by mistake, weren't aimed or nothing. That's what the men told me. Wasn't even the Klan shot him. It was someone from our side." Even as he said it, Luke realized how bad the truth sounded in this instance. He hung his head.

"Makes it all the worse, Luke. If there hadn't been guns, there would have been no shooting. Every man who picks up a gun contributes to the potential for death and injury. And a man who is so careless with a gun that it goes off accidentally . . ."

"But our men have to defend themselves."

Pa shook his head as though he were very tired and very discouraged. "We should be able to defend ourselves by reason, not force."

"But," Luke protested, "you can't reason with people like that. They wouldn't have listened if someone told them Canton was not their town and asked them politely to leave."

"Did the sheriff say that?"

"Sheriff Browder?" Luke looked surprised. "I don't know what he did, but Mr. Jones said this morning he thought the sheriff was probably hiding under a desk. Isn't that right, Theo?"

I wasn't anxious to be drawn into this conversation, but I nodded.

"It was the sheriff's place to order those men out of town . . . or arrest them," Pa said firmly.

"How could he?" Luke asked impatiently. "Just walk up and say real nice, 'You're under arrest?' They'd probably shoot him."

"Not," Pa muttered, "if the man would act like he has authority. Or at least send for federal troops to help."

Luke looked at the floor so hard that Pa noticed. "He didn't send for help, did he, Luke?"

"No, sir," he mumbled. "Mr. Clintlock told him not to. Said we don't want soldiers up here. We'll take care of things ourselves."

Pa held his head in his hands and said no more, but I could tell he was angry and worried. I was torn between their two points of view, but mostly I could see that Pa was right. It wouldn't do any good to make a bad situation worse by fighting, even if you couldn't reason with the Klan.

Finally, Pa spoke, but it was just to tell us good night and that he thought we all needed some sleep. Luke announced he couldn't sleep yet and wanted to just sit out in the night air.

"Luke," Pa said very solemnly, "I have to ask you not to go back to town tonight."

Luke looked startled, then dropped his eyes. "I . . . I got to."

"No, Luke, you don't. I forbid it."

"You . . ." Luke stammered for words, and Pa went on.

"I know I have no legal right to forbid, but once before I relied on your good judgment, and you let me down. This time, I forbid it. As long as you live in my house, you will obey me."

"Yessir," Luke bit his lips and looked down, and even I ached for him.

Pa softened his tone and put an arm around Luke. "I know you can't understand or believe this, but it's for your own good, Luke, your own safety. I'm not ordering you to stay home just so you can cotton to my beliefs. I'm concerned about you . . . and I don't want you near a fight."

But Luke wasn't ready to be pacified. He shrugged off Pa's arm and left the room. It was the first and only time I ever saw him be rude to Pa, but I guess Pa understood. He let Luke go without a word.

I followed him, and we sat on the dogtrot. We must have been there another hour or more. Somehow, my desperate need for sleep was gone, and I, too, wanted to talk, as though talking would help me puzzle things out.

"My pa, he taught me to stand up for what's mine. An eye for an eye, he said. If someone hits you, you hit back. If someone takes what's yours, you get it back. And you do whatever you have to."

"Pa believes in turning the other cheek," I said slowly. "I

mean, he stands up for what's his, but he believes in doing it peacefully. There's so much senseless violence. That was what Pa thought about the whole war. It was senseless that so many men were hurt and killed."

"I can see that, Theo, but it's like I'm honor-bound now . . . those men are counting on me."

"For what?"

Now he was vague. "I don't know. Whatever they need."

"What if you got hurt . . . or even killed." It scared me some to say it.

"I ain't gonna get hurt."

"That's what everyone thinks. You know what Pa would say, Luke? I can hear him say it's bad enough those men want to fight fire with fire, but it's unbelievable they would involve someone your age."

His tone was quickly belligerent. "I'm old enough."

"That's not what Pa says. He says you think of a fight as an adventure . . . and he knows better from The War."

Luke was silent a long while, and I thought probably he was offended by what I said, but that wasn't how he sounded when he finally spoke again. "What did happen to him in the war?" he asked.

"He was wounded," I said, digging up that old memory of my father limping home in a tattered uniform. "Shot in the hip. He didn't talk about it much, but he was in an army hospital a long time . . . and I guess all the suffering he saw there convinced him that there should never be war. When he first came home, he looked . . . oh, I don't know, haunted, like a ghost, and I heard him tell my mother he could still hear men screaming to die so their pain would end."

"War was hard on everyone," Luke said defensively, "but my pa would have said that's the price you pay for freedom. 'Course, he wasn't in the war. He wasn't in it, but he sympathized with the South. Said they were having their rights invaded, and it was a noble thing to defend them. Just like it's a noble adventure to defend your own county."

"Your pa," I said, with a touch of bitterness, "but he's not here, and my pa is."

"Theo, I admire your pa almost more than any other man. More in lots of ways than my own pa. I know he shouldn't have just ridden off and left me. It was a weak thing to do. But he's still my pa, and I still got to do what he'd have me do. It's . . . oh, I can't explain it right."

"I guess I understand, Luke." I was too tired from thinking and worrying to talk about it any more. "Night."

"Night."

I went to bed, filled with dread for what the next day would bring.

Surprisingly, the next day brought no drama or tragedy, though it started off badly enough. I woke up late to a quiet, calm morning, and it took me a minute to recollect the events of the night before. But then I dressed in a hurry, desperate to see if Luke was still home and what had happened during the night.

Luke was there all right, cross as a bear, and no one mentioned any excitement during the night. I was afraid to ask, so I just went about fixing the breakfast. Luke and I tangled even before I got breakfast on the table. I handed him a bowl of oatmeal, and he dropped it on the floor, breaking the bowl and splattering me with hot cereal. He made a terrific mess.

"Luke, why are you so clumsy?" I, too, was cross, mostly from lack of sleep, and my tone was far from pleasant.

"Why'd you hand me a bowl that was too hot to touch?"

"It wasn't too hot. I was holding it, wasn't I?"

"You got hands of iron, just like your tongue."

"I suspect both of you would be better off to clean it up,"

Pa said quietly, walking into the room. "And do try to keep your voices down. Mr. Hanson is awake and in pain."

As usual, Pa didn't have to scold us. His quiet tone was punishment for both of us, and we slunk to the task of cleaning up the oatmeal. I fixed Luke another bowl and set it carefully in front of him. He mumbled his thanks without looking me in the eye.

"Luke, have you got a chicken ready to kill?"

Luke looked surprised at Pa's question, but he answered right away. "Sure."

"I think chicken soup would benefit Mr. Hanson. Theo can boil up a big pot."

"Isn't it kind of hot for soup?" I wasn't exactly eager to boil a hen and heat up the cabin that much, what with the all-day fire it would take.

"Yes, it is, for us, Theo. But Mr. Hanson won't be able to hold much else on his stomach, and he needs nourishment."

"Yes, Pa."

"I'll get the hen right after breakfast," Luke said.

"Good. I'll pretty much need you to tend to Mr. Hanson today."

Luke looked downcast, and I knew he was wishing desperately that he was in town, or that he at least knew what had happened. I still thought it was real strange we hadn't heard any noise, no gunfire, no fighting.

Luke's unspoken questions were answered a bit later by the arrival of Mr. Jones.

"Came to check on Hanson, Doc."

"He's in quite a bit of pain, Mr. Jones, but doing as well as I could hope. Too soon to tell much about it."

"When you gonna know if he's gonna keep that foot?"

"Within a few days, I should think. Meantime, I'll keep him here. How are things in town?" Pa had never shown any of the raging curiosity that tore at Luke and me. I privately wondered how he could be so calm about the possible fight in town.

"Those cowards left during the night. Snuck away!"

I was open-mouthed for a minute, then went out to the

chicken house in search of Luke, who was singling out a chicken for slaughter.

"Luke! They left."

"Who left?" His disgusted tone told me he had neither forgiven me for our spat this morning nor gotten over Pa's order that he stay home.

"The Klan. Mr. Jones is here, and he says those men left during the night."

"They did?" Now he forgot to be angry. "No trouble? No fight?"

"Guess not. They must have left too soon."

I think Luke was part relieved, part disappointed, but I was wholeheartedly relieved.

Mr. Hanson stayed with us for nearly two weeks, and we came to know him pretty well. He was a dirt patch farmer trying to grow cotton on a little place several miles south of town. He loved the land and, once he was in less pain, told me stories of the Indians who used to live in Van Zandt County and of Cynthia Ann Parker, the famous white captive who had lived nearby with her Indian daughter. One story I really liked was about Ben Wheeler, the mailman who refused to carry mail for the Confederacy. He said as a carrier of the mails he'd taken an oath to support the U.S. Constitution. I guessed he was like a lot of people in this county, holding back from supporting the Confederacy, and even though I thought he was on the wrong side, I admired his honesty.

It was from Mr. Hanson, too, that I learned more about the Klan and what had really happened that day. Seems, as

Pa suspected, the Klansmen rode in to demonstrate their strength.

"Showing off, they were," Mr. Hanson said. "And whiskied up but good."

"Drunk?" I asked incredulously. I probably never heard of a whole group of men being drunk together. I knew about Old Bill McAdam in Green City, who drank himself senseless and got put in jail at least once a week, and even proper Miss Thetford who sipped sherry all day long. But this was different. A whole group of men drunk in the middle of the day.

"Yes, Miss Theo, they were drunk. And rowdy. That's how come I got shot. They were plain just showing off, fooling with their guns when they didn't have their wits about them. It was an accident, sure enough."

"But, Luke said one of our . . . one of your friends shot you."

"No, miss, it was a Klansman. And that first shot was accidental. But once they shot me, they got carried away with themselves a little and held their guns on us, forcing us to stay in that bank. No sense arguing with a drunk who's holding a rifle. We didn't even have any guns."

"Wonder why they left in the middle of the night?"

He almost chuckled. "Maybe they ran out of whisky." Then he got more serious. "Maybe they knew we was planning a fight."

His use of the word "we" didn't go by me. I knew Mr. Hanson was a member of the Van Zandt Army, such as it was.

"I'm downright mad," he went on, "that we missed a chance to whip those yellow-livered cowards."

I liked Mr. Hanson well enough to hope he didn't talk to Pa that way.

Every day Mr. Hanson's wife came to visit, bringing with her a treat for our dining table. She was a plump, happy lady, and I learned more about cooking from her in a week than I'd have learned by myself in ten years. One day she'd bring a dried fruit pie and the next it was rice and beans cooked together and carried in a big pot. Her cornbread was light and delicious, with a hint of sweet taste, and Luke thought it a great improvement over mine, which tended to be dry and tasteless.

"Nothing to it, dearie," she assured me. "You just put in a good dose of honey. I'll bring you some. Got me some bees and I get good fresh honey."

"Mrs. Hanson, you're spoiling us."

She turned serious. "No, I'm just trying to say thank you. Your pa saved my man's foot and there ain't . . . isn't no way we can repay you. We don't have much money, but we keep ourselves and our kin well fed. No reason we can't share it with you."

After that, I accepted her gifts gratefully and without complaint. I knew Pa and Luke were glad to have a respite from my cooking.

When Pa finally told Mr. Hanson he could go home, it was a great day for them but a sad one for us. I had enjoyed both of them more than I realized, but I knew Mrs. Hanson was anxious to have him back home. It was hard on her to tend to her bees and her vegetables and all and still spend time at our cabin with her husband.

Pa had talked to Mr. Hanson about his limp, and he'd accepted it well. Now he promised to keep off the foot until Pa said he could test it and to watch carefully for any sign of infection.

"I'll take good care of him, you can count on that," Mrs. Hanson assured Pa.

"She'll be bothering me all the time," her husband said with a grin. "Doc, you tell her I need peace and quiet. No talking." He leaned on his crutches, smiling at her, then turned his head in my direction. "Miss Theo, you can come out to the farm—Luke can bring you—and I'll tell you some more of them stories. Still got lots left."

"Thank you, I'll do that . . . if Luke'll bring me."

"Yeah, I guess." Luke didn't seem overjoyed, but he shook hands with Mr. Hanson, and I thought Mr. Hanson kind of winked at him, as though they shared a secret.

The rest of the summer we heard rumors of the Klan's activities to the south of us, but we had no more visits from them. Their seige of the courthouse had its longlasting effect, though. The men of Van Zandt County were ready for a fight. Pa talked to me about it one night when we were alone, as we often were lately. Luke was probably up at The Clancey Inn.

"I don't like it, Theo. There's going to be trouble. Somehow when men set their sights on trouble and then it fails to materialize, they often go looking for it anywhere they can find it."

"You mean, they were robbed of their fight with the Klan?"

"Exactly. And now they've got to get rid of that energy somehow."

"Luke's involved, isn't he?"

"Luke sees things differently than I do. We've talked about it, and he, well, he explained to me about his father. But I wish I could convince him." Pa began to pace as he talked. "I talked with Jones today. He's one of the leaders, you know, and he was talking about how the Klan is partly responsible for the military government." He turned toward me, with an almost desperate look on his face and anguish in his voice. "It's not logical, Theo. Texas is under military rule because . . . well, because of that damn War, not some hooded hooligans in white robes."

Pa's talk was getting too complicated for me, but I knew he felt seriously about it because he said "damn" which was a word he hardly ever used.

"President Johnson has declared the rebellion in Texas at an end officially," Pa went on.

"Is that good?" I ventured.

"Certainly it's good. It clears the way for Texas to rejoin the Union." Pa said this with great determination. "But I'm afraid there are some around here that won't see it that way. You mark my words. There'll be trouble in this county."

7

PA'S WORDS were prophetic, as we found out in the fall. If I had been surprised by the bloom and freshness of spring in East Texas, I was equally taken with the cool clearness of fall, with trees that turned to red and gold and soft temperatures cool enough that I didn't mind heating up the stove and cooking supper. The breeze that rustled the tops of the pines didn't yet have a hint of winter in it, and I fooled myself into thinking that fall, and peaceful days, would last forever.

The Klan and threats of violence seemed far away, and my thoughts and time were wholly occupied with school. I had always enjoyed it back home and had missed classes sorely the last year when I didn't attend. Pa talked to the teacher when we arrived in the spring, but she said school was nearly over for this year and there was no sense my starting so late. Miss Sullivan, that was her name, gave Pa some books for me, and I'd been reading all summer.

But I was a little scared of a new school and new classmates. Except for Luke and Lucille Johnson, who'd come to see me early in the spring, I did not know one other person my age.

"It'll be all right, Theo. Just don't try to boss them the way you do me." Luke grinned and danced away from the foot I aimed at his shins.

Luke was not nearly as happy about returning to school. He, too, had been out the last year, and he'd gotten out of the habit of school. He insisted that he could learn doctoring, as he still called it, better by following Pa around than by going back to school where they concentrated on how neat your handwriting was and how much twelve times twelve equalled. Pa was amused at him and probably would have preferred to have his company all winter long, but he held firm and told Luke he expected him to attend school every day and to do his lessons carefully.

So Luke and I began classes together in the fall. There were only fifteen students, but even so the small frame schoolhouse was crowded. We sat on long wooden benches for reading, and there were six desks at which we took turns to do our arithmetic. Miss Sullivan had the imagination to brighten the walls with pictures from *Harper's Weekly* which she used for geography lessons and advertisement posters which she used for arithmetic. I was pleased to be one of the oldest students and also one of the most advanced, and when it fell my lot to help Luke with his reading, I resolved not to be condescending.

"What's that word, Theo?"

"Sound it out, Luke. Start with the p . . ."

"Per . . . kep . . ."

"Perceptions, Luke, perceptions."

"What's it mean?"

"Look it up in the dictionary."

He gave me a black look and walked over to the huge dictionary that stood on a stand in one corner of the room.

On the playground, I got to know the other students and soon was accepted into their games and, somewhat later, into their conversations. We girls jumped rope while the boys played marbles in a ring in the dirt and batted an India rubber ball about. As long as the weather was good, we ate our lunches under a big, old hackberry tree.

Schoolyard talk was all about Texas being voted back into

the Union and the contest of ballots then going on in the State Capitol.

"My pa says if they force us back into the Union, there'll be trouble all over Texas," said Clayton Clintlock, the mayor's son. Obviously, I thought, he's been listening to his father.

"Sure will," chimed in another. "They can't force us to forget secession and all that. We didn't do anything wrong around here, and we ain't responsible for what the rest of the state did."

"My father thinks it will be progress," I said, freely entering the discussion, since I'd come to feel at home with my classmates.

There was a moment of silence, during which several incredulous faces turned toward me.

"Your pa!" scoffed Clayton, "He doesn't believe in fighting."

Face burning, I searched for the proper answer, but Luke was faster than me.

"That's right," Luke said vehemently, "he doesn't believe in fighting . . . and he's got every right to his own ideas. Just so happens he may be right."

"You of all people!" laughed another boy. "How can you say it's not right to fight when you're the official mascot of the Van Zandt troops?"

"I ain't exactly official," Luke mumbled, "and besides, Doc Burford's been explaining it some to me, and lots of what he says makes sense. If we go back into the Union, we'll have one authority, instead of having a governor and a military government that keep cancelling each other out."

"Well," put in Lucille, "the governor's all right. My ma says he's pure Texan. It's those outsiders we got to watch." Then, blushing, she looked right at me and whispered, "Not you, Theo. I don't think you're an outsider any more."

Somehow I found her reassurance more upsetting than ever, and I sat silent, out of the conversation.

On the way home, I asked Luke why he had come to Pa's defense.

"Why wouldn't I? I told you before, Theo, but you don't

listen. I admire your pa almost more than any other man, and I won't sit by and listen to him criticized."

"But you don't agree with him about violence?"

"Maybe I do, and maybe I don't. I been thinking about it, and he's right that it feeds on itself. If you don't start a fight, the other fellow has less cause to fight. And if you don't fight back, he can't fight all by himself."

"But you're still involved with Arley Clintlock's wild scheme."

"That's different," he said, but his voice was kind of weak, as though he didn't believe it.

"Luke Widman, I think Pa was right. You like the excitement, and it makes you important at school and all." I flounced away from him and walked the rest of the way home silently. Somehow, I wanted Luke to be more noble than to be drawn into a scraggly local army because it gave him prestige.

Things went on quite calmly. Pa's practice was busier than ever, and Luke and I were precious little help to him, both busy with school and our chores around the cabin. It was all I could do to keep up with the housework and my homework, too, and some nights it was late and I was dog-tired before I lay down on my rough slat bed. On Saturdays, I generally had to work hard to make up for the things I hadn't gotten done during the week, like the washing, and sometimes I even had to work on the Sabbath. Pa frowned if he saw me heat the wash pot when I came home from church, and I tried to get it all done before Sunday but many weeks there was just too much.

One Saturday, I was hanging laundry out behind the cabin when Luke came down the road, calling in great excitement, "Theo, Theo, they've done it!"

"Who's done what?" I asked irritably. What a dumb way for him to say hello.

"They've called a town meeting. Mr. Clintlock and them, they've posted bulletins all over town."

"Town meeting? What for?"

He regarded me as though I were dumber than dumb. "To talk about our government, of course. We're tired of a government that can't do anything and of being pushed around by outsiders."

"Well, what can you do about it?" I truly didn't see what good meeting and talking about it would do.

"You'll see, you'll see," Luke said exultantly.

Pa always seemed to come up behind us when Luke or I didn't want him to. This time he looked kind of stern. "What's this about a town meeting, Luke?"

"Mr. Clintlock called one for Tuesday night at sundown. You'll go, won't you?"

Pa raised one eyebrow. "No, Luke, I most certainly will not. I'm not involved in local politics . . . and I am not in agreement with some sentiments that are now popular around here."

"But, sir, if this were Mississippi . . ."

"This is not Mississippi," Pa said firmly, ending the discussion.

Luke and I sat out on the dogtrot later that night. It was chilly and I shivered a little even with a shawl wrapped around my shoulders.

"Smells like fall, doesn't it?" I asked conversationally. "Have you noticed the sweet-gums? They turn such a brilliant red."

"Yeah." Obviously, his mind was somewhere other than on sweet-gum trees.

"What's the matter, Luke?"

"Oh, nothin' . . . it's just, well, never mind."

"Luke!"

"Okay, okay. I wish your pa would go to that meeting.

Maybe then he'd understand why some of the men feel the way they do. You know, Theo, in some ways it's like he's blind on certain subjects."

I felt I should leap to Pa's defense again, yet in a way I agreed with Luke. If we were going to live here, Pa ought to take part in things. "I guess he just doesn't want to be part of actions he doesn't approve of."

"But, Theo, remember when we talked about the U.S. Constitution in school last week? The whole point was that everybody should have a voice in things. Your pa should go to that meeting to stand up for whatever he believes."

I wanted to change the subject. It isn't easy to see a big chink in your own pa. "Are you going to the meeting?"

Luke grinned. "It's just for the men, Theo. I can't go. But I'll be around."

"Can I go with you?"

He was shocked. "Of course not. It's no place for girls." The scorn in his voice was too evident.

Before I could protest, Pa came to the door of his study. "Have you two finished your lessons?"

We chorused the word "yes" but Pa wasn't satisfied. "Luke, let me go over your arithmetic with you. Theo, I'm sure you could practice your penmanship."

"Yes, Pa."

Luke didn't mention the meeting again, but by Tuesday I had made up my mind that I, too, was going to know what went on. I kind of hurried Luke and Pa through supper that night so I could get to the cleaning up.

"I ain't even finished my supper, Theo. For land's sake, give me my plate."

"You sure are slow," I said peevishly.

Pa sided with Luke. "You do seem to be rushing us some, Theo. What's the problem?"

"Oh, nothing, Pa. I . . . I just got a lot of lessons to do tonight."

Pa was so set on education that he'd give up anything, even eat his dinner in a hurry, for the sake of my studying. I felt guilty lying to him, but I was determined. And I was tired of Luke knowing everything I didn't.

Finally, I had the kitchen mess cleaned up, and Pa was settled in his study. Luke had disappeared without my noticing it, but I knew full well where he'd gone. It was well after sundown, which was the time the meeting was called for, and I knew I had to hurry. I set the lamp at the table I had just cleared, so Pa would think I was studying. With any luck at all, Pa would still be working in his study when I came home, and he'd think I was doing my lessons all the while. If a patient came, however . . . I refused to think about that possibility.

Quiet as I could, I stepped out the door and off the dogtrot. Soon as I was a ways away from the cabin, I broke into a run and didn't stop until I was out of breath, nearly to the old log courthouse where the meeting was. Light glowed out the windows and through cracks in the walls, and even at a distance I could hear the murmur of men talking. I thought about it a minute, then chose a window for my vantage point. Sticking to the shadows and edges of the buildings, I made my way to the far side of the building where one window was a little lower than the others. Whoever built that awful old building hadn't had enough sense to get the windows even, but this night I was glad.

Standing on tiptoe, I could grasp the windowsill and peek over just enough to get a glimpse. The room was crowded with men in dirty workclothes, men who'd been working all day, some of whom had come a fair distance from the far corners of the county for this meeting. They muttered and mumbled among themselves, but it was Mr. Clintlock, still dressed in his spotless city suit, who held the floor.

"If we go back into the Union, we'll still face all the problems of Reconstruction . . . and you gentlemen know what that means. The problems of the South will be visited upon us, even though we're not involved. We'll have more Klan visits up here . . . and we'll have the militia, court martials and all that. No peace at all."

I couldn't follow his logic. To me, if they went back into the Union, the militia would be withdrawn and once that happened, the Klan might well disappear. But I supposed Mr. Clintlock knew more about it than I did.

"What'll happen if we withdraw?" asked one grizzled old man who raised a bony hand in the air to get Mr. Clintlock's attention.

"Well," the banker hedged, "we don't quite know for sure . . . but self-government is our right. We cannot let ourselves be forced into accepting a government that doesn't work for us."

The room echoed with cries of "Hear, hear!" and Mr. Clintlock looked real pleased with himself.

"War, that's what'll happen," yelled a young man I'd never seen before. "And we'll be ready for them!"

Again there was a string of shouts and hollers. It seemed most of the men thought war was a good idea. I was glad Pa hadn't listened to Luke and had stayed home. He'd have been horrified, and even I felt awful uneasy.

I had to stand flat on the ground for a few seconds to rest, but the swelling chorus of noise inside intrigued me so I was back up on my tiptoes pretty quick. But I didn't get to see much before I felt myself jerked back away from the window by an unseen hand behind me.

Terrified, I almost screamed aloud. In that brief second, I wondered if they still shot spies. Then I heard a familiar voice.

"Theo Burford, what're you doing here?" He was whispering but even so, it was plain that Luke was absolutely furious with me.

"Luke Widman, you scared me!" I accused, forgetting to whisper.

He clapped a hand over my mouth quick. "Shhh. Don't you have any brains? You're not supposed to be here."

"Neither are you," I shot back, pushing his hand from my mouth.

All the time, Luke was pulling me away from the courthouse until we were far enough into the shadows that we could neither be seen nor heard.

"Stop pulling me."

"I ought to whip you."

"Ha! You're not big enough." His superior attitude was really making me mad.

"Theo," he said, trying to be more patient. "I told you this was no place for girls. Do you even see one woman in there?"

I shook my head and avoided looking at him.

"That's because this is men's business. And you of all people. You'll probably run tell your pa just what they decide."

"No, I won't," I said stubbornly, "and if you don't let me go back, we'll neither one know what they do decide."

"We already know, and no, you're not going back there. We're both going home."

"Don't trouble yourself on my account," I said huffily. "I can go home alone."

"I don't trust you," he replied. "Let's go."

We walked in silence most of the way, me marching angrily a few steps ahead of Luke who wasn't exactly pleased himself.

"All right," I said when we were almost to the cabin. "I promise to go home. It wasn't such an exciting old meeting anyway. You go on."

"No, it's too late. I . . . your pa will be wondering where I am."

"I hope he isn't wondering where we both are," I said fervently.

Pa was still working as far as we could tell, and Luke followed me into the other side of the cabin. It was too cool for one of our long evenings on the dogtrot.

"Luke, why did you say we already know what will happen at that meeting?"

He settled himself at the table and opened a book, at least putting up the appearance of working on his studies. "It's obvious just from what the men have said. They feel they're being pushed around, and they resent it. They'll vote to withdraw from the State of Texas."

"How can they?" My mind boggled at the idea.

"Guess they just do it. Why can't they?"

"Who would govern us?"

"We'd have our own government. I don't know much about that, Theo . . . I don't guess they've thought too far beyond what happens after they secede."

Secession! It would be The Great War all over again, just on a smaller scale. How could Van Zandt County be an independent state or country when it was completely surrounded by Texas? Surrounded was putting it mildly. Van Zandt County was buried in the heart of East Texas. And no one county could fight a successful war against the whole U.S. government. I was terrified by the possibilities that Luke didn't even seem to see. To him, as Pa said and I now saw, it was all a great and glorious adventure. To me, it was folly. Suddenly, I saw myself aligned with my father.

But my fears were momentarily lightened by a wild thought that sent me into a giggle. "Luke, can you see Mr. Clintlock as President of the Country of Van Zandt?"

Luke giggled too, and we both looked up to see Pa standing in the doorway.

By now, I was less worried over my own guilt about sneaking away than I was over what Pa's reaction would be when he heard the news. Trying to be bright and cheerful, I avoided the moment. "Through working, Pa? Want some coffee?"

He looked somber. "No, thank you. I do have something to say to both of you. I would not want either of you ever to tell me an untruth, tempted though you might be, so I won't ask where you were tonight. But I would like to know the decision of the town meeting."

I didn't know whether to laugh or cry. Pa was so gentle in his reprimand that I felt worse than ever, like crying, but he was so clever in trapping us that I wanted to grin in appreciation. I did neither.

"There was no decision," Luke said without looking the least embarrassed. "Far as I know, they're still talking."

"But you can tell something from the tone of the meeting."

"Yeah."

"Luke!" Even Pa, who never lost his temper, was getting exasperated. "Do I have to drag it out of you?"

"No, sir. They'll vote for independence."

Pa shook his head sadly. "It's wrong," he said. "It's the worst thing they could do." And he turned on his heel and left us.

The meeting did indeed vote to declare Van Zandt County independent of the State of Texas and the United States. Within twenty-four hours, hastily printed notices went up on trees throughout the county, proclaiming the independence and declaring a temporary governing body of men from the several small towns around. Mr. Clintlock, of course, and Jones the butcher represented Canton.

Luke talked to me about it as we walked home from school.

"Your pa should be on that board, Theo. If only he'd have gone to that meeting."

"Pa wants no part of it . . . and I think he's right," I said staunchly.

"He may be. That's why he should be there. He's the best educated, smartest man in the county, and they need him." He kicked at a rock and stared off into the distance.

How could I disagree with that assessment of Pa?

"Luke, what will happen next? The government won't just let us secede, will they? Will there really be a war?" I hated even to say the word.

"Not like you're thinking of, Theo." He must have read my thoughts, for he really tried to be comforting. "But there'll be trouble. We're ready for them. Don't worry."

"What about you?"

"What about me?"

"I . . . I don't want you to get hurt."

For once, Luke looked embarrassed, staring down at the ground. "I thought I was just a pain in your life."

"You are," I answered as smart as I could, "but I still don't want to get rid of you that way."

"Thanks a bunch, Theo. Well, you don't need to worry. I ain't gonna get hurt. It won't be that kind of a war, I don't think."

"When will we know?"

"Well, nobody's exactly gonna rush off and tell Sheridan what we did, so he'll have to find out. That could take a couple of weeks or longer. Then he'll have to organize some outfit to send up here . . . another week. Then it'll take them a week or so to get here. Might be nothing happen for a month."

"You mean we have to just sit and wait for a whole month?"

"Yep, we have to wait."

We had reached the cabin by then, and our conversation

ended. I thought surely I would burst from suspense in a month, but we settled down, in anxiety, to see what General Phil Sheridan would do. Luke's prediction was right. It was exactly a month before we knew anything.

8

"LUKE WIDMAN! Where've you been? The stove needs wood and it's right cool in here." My temper was as short as my words. Luke really hadn't had a chance to get wood because he'd just come in from making a call with Pa. We both knew I was jumping him for no reason at all. He just threw me a dirty look and said, "Yes, ma'am," real sarcastically. I guess the strain of waiting to see what General Sheridan would do was telling on all of us.

It had been a month to the day since the meeting at the log courthouse, and in that time a temporary government had been set up for Van Zandt County. It didn't function very well. Matter of fact, I couldn't see much of anything they did, except Mr. Clintlock swaggered around very important since he was chosen temporary president by the representatives from the small towns. He even made a glowing speech one Saturday morning in front of the courthouse about improving life in Van Zandt County. There was a passing reference to schools and maybe reestablishing a newspaper but the main emphasis was on safety.

All the men and half the women in Canton including Luke and me but not Pa stood around listening as though he was saying something new and original. I guess he was what you call a powerful speaker because everybody believed him.

"Van Zandt Co . . . I mean, the State of Van Zandt will be known far and wide as a place where citizens can live in peace and harmony, without the dissent and discord that bothers our brothers in the State of Texas," he preached.

"Doesn't he think war with Sheridan's troops will bring 'dissent and discord'?" I asked mockingly, which earned me another of Luke's black looks and an elbow in my ribs.

"Theo, be quiet and listen," he whispered.

"I've heard enough," I said and headed for home. Each day I was filled with dread and fear at the thought of another war. I couldn't imagine Van Zandt County's fine protectors waging a war anything like the great war we'd just come through, but still, the whole idea sickened me.

The expected war was all the kids at school talked about, too. The boys played war games, though they were hard put to get someone to play the part of Sheridan, and the girls spent endless hours speculating on when the troops would arrive, how big a troop and so on. Some of the girls my age and older wondered if the federal soldiers were young and good-looking. I was an outsider in these conversations because everyone knew about Pa and, besides, it showed that I outright resented the idea of war. I didn't care if the soldiers were good-looking and I didn't think the men of Van Zandt were wonderful and brave. I thought they were foolish. I resented the idea of war for lots of reasons—because of Pa, and most I guess, though I never admitted it, because I was worried about Luke.

I was worried about Pa, too. He spent all his time working at his desk in that tiny office these days. Few patients came to see him, and Mr. Clintlock made the reason clear one day when he came to see Pa. I listened openly that time.

"They think you're not in favor of the State of Van Zandt. Not quite a traitor . . ." Mr. Clintlock let his voice trail off.

Pa shook his head sadly. "They are the traitors . . . to themselves. Why can you people not see reason?"

"Now, Doc, we're being reasonable . . . and we're trying our darndest to get you to do the same. Ain't . . . I mean we aren't asking you to bear arms. I know you're against that. But show some support for our new arrangement hereabouts."

"That's just it. How can I support a new government, flimsy as this piece of paper, when I know that another violent clash is inevitable?" He paused, the piece of paper he'd grabbed hanging limply from his hand. "You know, it's not too late. You could send a message to Sheridan . . . or simply walk out and meet his troops when they arrive."

"Never! I can see you don't understand a thing about this, sir." Mr. Clintlock got real formal, trying to be dignified, I guess.

"You're right, I don't understand. But let me ask you . . . don't you understand that you are putting these people right back into a state of rebellion? Just when the rebellion has been declared over?"

"This is a rebellion for the proper reasons," our banker leader said kind of haughtily.

They ended their discussion soon, since neither of them was getting anywhere, and Pa went back to his work. I began to suspect he was writing a history of some kind or maybe something about the virtues of non-violence.

"Coffee, Pa?" I asked softly, wishing in some way I could comfort him.

"What? Oh, no thanks, Theo." He went on writing, and I got the feeling he didn't even know if I'd left the room.

Our suspense ended, or perhaps began again, that evening. Luke, who'd been sent back to town for the schoolbooks he'd conveniently forgotten, came bursting in, more excited than I'd ever seen him.

"They're coming, Theo! They're really coming!"

I didn't need to ask who. It was Sheridan's troops. "How . . . do you know?" I stammered.

"Oh," he answered scornfully, "we've had riders posted for two weeks now. Ol' Tim Johnson came riding in not fifteen minutes ago. Says they're marching near Tyler, be here tomorrow if they camp as we expect."

A cold lump of terror stuck in my throat and all I could manage was a whispered, "Oh."

"Now, Theo." Luke was patient and concerned. "Don't be such a worrywart. We're ready for them. The Free State of Van Zandt is gonna triumph."

It sounded like a fearful battle cry to me and in my sudden feeling of sickness, I felt the urge to do something, anything, so I busied myself setting the table, slamming knives and forks harder than I meant. Luke watched in silence for a bit, then he spoke very deliberately.

"Theo, you got to promise me something."

I just looked at him.

"There'll be no school tomorrow—it's official—and I want you to stay in the cabin all day. Mr. Clintlock, he's ordering all women and children behind locked doors until he pro . . . pro . . ."

"Pronounces?"

"Yeah, that's it. Pronounces it safe. But Theo, one more thing."

"It isn't enough I have to stay cooped up in this cabin? Where will you be?"

"I don't know for sure," he said evasively. "But you got to promise that your pa won't go making any calls on these country roads."

Pa's safety hadn't ever occurred to me. I just assumed he wouldn't be part of the fracas, yet now Luke was giving me a new worry. "Nobody calls him much anymore," I said bitterly, "so you probably don't have to worry. But you know Pa. If someone needs him, he'll go."

"Yeah. I guess I'll talk to him, though."

I reckon that was the hardest thing Luke Widman ever had to do, but he went right out the door and over to Pa's study. I heard him knock and say softly, "Can I, uh, talk to you a minute, sir?" Then, of course, like always, they closed the door, and I was left out again.

This time, much to my surprise, Pa told me what they talked about. It was the next morning as I fixed breakfast.

"Theo, Luke has told me the so-called battle plan, if it can be called that, and I think it's important that we talk about it."

"Yes, Pa."

"Do you remember studying about the Revolutionary War?"

I couldn't fathom why Pa was talking about that long ago war when I was impatient to hear about the present, but I wracked my brain for the little I remembered. It wasn't much. "Yes, a little," I said uncertainly.

"Do you remember how the Americans beat the British, even though they were outnumbered by men better equipped and more experienced in fighting?"

"Not exactly," I admitted.

"Well, they took advantage of their own knowledge of the land. They hid in trees and took pot-shots at the approaching British troops. The British soldiers marched in formation as they always did, and they didn't know the land well enough to find these farmers who were perched in trees, hidden behind bushes, lying in ditches, scattered everywhere. The British never knew when to expect a bullet, and even the suspense took its toll."

I just waited patiently for Pa to get to the point of what this had to do with the State of Van Zandt.

"The terrain here is suited to just such a tactic, and it's what the so-called army of Van Zandt plans to do."

"Take pot-shots?"

"Yes. They'll hide in trees and forests and attack bit by bit before the troops ever get far across the county line."

"Is that good?"

Pa shook his head unhappily. "Of course it's not good. But

I guess it's better than meeting the troops outright in an old-fashioned pitched battle. It'll give our men more of a chance.

It took me a minute to realize Pa had used the word "our" —maybe he felt more a part of Van Zandt than I'd realized. At least, he was holding out hope for Luke.

"That's why Luke urged us to stay inside all day. No one knows from which direction the troops will come, though I suspect it will be straight up from Tyler, and you can't be sure where the fighting will be. I have assured Luke we will remain in the cabin." He rose from the chair as though indicating that was all he had to say.

"Pa?"

"Yes, Theo?"

I had a burning question on my mind, and also a strong desire to continue this conversation. It was the first time in months that Pa had actually talked to me at any length. "What about Luke? Is he going to have to stay home, too?"

Pa sank into the seat again. "No, Theo, I have not forbidden him to join the army."

"Pa!" It was an anguished cry on my part. "How could you?"

"I ordered Luke to stay home once before, and it was a mistake. It made no difference in his thinking. He has to be free . . . to do what he thinks is important."

"He's too young to decide that," I cried from my vantage point of fourteen years.

"No, Theo, both you children are old beyond your years because of your experiences. I have not had to face this same kind of dilemma with you, but I may soon, and Luke has helped me know how to react. I cannot order him to my ways. He must come of his own accord . . . and I still have hope." His voice was tinged with resignation as he added, "But not for today."

That day was probably the longest one either Pa or I ever spent. No one came to see Pa, of course, and for once, he seemed not to be able to work on his writing project. He'd get up and pace back and forth on the dogtrot, or go out to look at Luke's chickens.

"Pa, Luke said you shouldn't be out of the house," I was a little apprehensive about correcting Pa, but then again, there was an uncleared field not far behind the chickens. Sheridan's troops could be lurking in those trees, for all I knew.

"Theo," Pa said impatiently, "it's perfectly safe to be around here. If there were trouble near here, believe me, you'd know it."

Rebuked, I went back into the house and tried to busy myself with embroidering a dress I'd made. It was a pale green merino dress, desperately needed for church as I had no good clothes left. I'd outgrown all the things Mama had instructed Nan to make for me, and now there was no Mama or Nan, just me to see to my own wardrobe. I didn't mind the sewing so much but I plain lacked Mama's taste in picking colors and designs. It was Mrs. Edgeworth at the mercantile store who suggested I embroider this one in a deeper shade of green thread. She was still raving about my stitches, and it flattered me enough that I decided to follow her suggestion.

But today I was all thumbs. No two stitches came out the same size, and it looked like a six-year-old had done her first piece of embroidery right there on the collar of my good dress. Frustrated, I put it aside and worked on a batch of bread. Kneading the dough kind of gave me an outlet for my energy and made me feel some better.

Outside, everything was still, almost too still. It was a clear, sunny day, warm for November, with hardly a breeze blowing. I suppose, looking back, I should have known the weather was preparing for a good, early winter storm in a few days, but all I could think was that it was too pretty a day for men to fight . . . and maybe die. I don't know what kind of noise I expected to hear—shouts, gunfire, lots of commotion I suppose—but I heard nothing. It seemed to me even the chickens were quieter than usual.

I was still kneading bread dough when Pa wandered into

111

the kitchen and sat at the round table. His expression was sad, and he was silent a long while before he asked,

"Is there any coffee, Theo?"

"Yes, Pa." I gave him a cup from the pot that sat on the still-warm stove. He murmured his thanks, sipping his coffee silently, and watching me as I shaped the loaves of bread and began cleaning up the floury mess I'd made.

For some reason, I, too, was quiet. Here it was, my always-wanted chance to talk with Pa alone, and yet I had no words. I don't know if it was the thought of Luke hanging between us or the distance that had developed over the past months or what. But ours was an uneasy silence, not the companionable one I would have liked. It was Pa who finally spoke first.

"You're much more capable than your mother, Theo. She never could learn to bake bread." He smiled a little as though he knew a funny story attached to his comment.

"She never had to bake bread, Pa. I guess if there was no one else to do it, Mama would have learned."

"I'm not so sure." Now he was grinning a little. "She tried one time. Insisted Nan teach her, but all she ended up with were some little tiny loaves so hard she could have used them to beat off mad dogs."

"I baked some that way, too, last spring. Didn't she try again?"

"No. As you say, she never had to bake the bread anyway." Silence hung over us for a minute again, then Pa said, "You're not quite living the kind of life your mother had in mind for you. And I suppose it's my fault."

I couldn't bear to have him feel guilty. "No, Pa, it's nobody's fault. Maybe the War's fault."

"Truthfully, Theo, I . . . well, I . . ." He rubbed his hand through his hair as though the words were difficult for him. "I do better with Luke than you." He sighed, as though glad he had it off his chest. I just stood staring. What did he mean by better?

"I don't know how to raise a girl. I never thought I'd have the responsibility. Your mama was the one to teach you the things girls should know. I guess maybe I thought being a girl came automatically."

"I'm doing all right," I said a bit defensively. "You just said so yourself when you talked about the bread baking."

"Yes, but you're missing something. The companionship of a woman, like you would have had if your mother lived. Now, Luke and I, we can be friends . . ."

I almost cried as I interrupted him. "Pa, don't you see? I'm not any different than Luke just because I'm a girl. I can be your friend, too. I want to. I really want to!"

He stared a minute, open-mouthed, and I turned away in embarrassment. But then Pa came over and put his arms around me, something he hadn't done in almost a year. I leaned against him and we stood there together, silent, until Pa spoke.

"I'll try to do better, Theo. It's been a hard year on both of us."

"Yes, Pa." As I moved away, I remembered something I wanted to ask. "Pa, what are you working on so hard in your office?"

"A history, Theo. Maybe no one but you will ever read it . . . you and Luke, probably . . . but I felt I had to write down my own interpretation of these days."

"I thought it was something like that. Don't you want other people to read it?"

"If they want to. But that's not why I'm writing it. I'm doing it selfishly, I guess . . . like I've done a lot of things lately."

"No, Pa, you're not selfish." I had to change the subject quick. "Pa, what about Luke. Will he be safe today?"

"That I can't tell you, Theo. Once the fighting starts, there's no telling what direction it will take."

"Don't you think we'd have heard some noise if they were fighting?"

"Not necessarily. Van Zandt County is a good-sized place, and they could be down to the south edge of the county. I expect they are."

"Oh."

Pa finally went back to his study, said he had to clean out some old medicines and stuff, and I busied myself around the cabin. I even thought about killing one of Luke's chickens to make a special supper for him, but I wasn't at all sure what suppertime would bring. Certainly, I didn't know if it would bring a hungry Luke. And besides, he'd be liable to get furious at me for having killed one of his chickens without permission. So I gave that idea up and started a pot of beans and rice.

After Pa and I had our talk, we both felt better, but our temporary calm shattered in the late afternoon when Pa came bursting into the cabin.

"Theo, did you hear that?"

"What?"

"Gunfire. Distant, but no mistake about it. I heard shots."

"Shots?" I felt dumb, but I was so scared all of a sudden that all I could do was echo what Pa was saying. Then way off I heard a little popping noise.

"There it is again, Theo. Closer this time!" Concern laced Pa's voice now, sending me even deeper into fright.

Silently we stood and listened, but there was no more sound. Pa walked out on the dogtrot to hear better, and I followed close on his heels. We stood there, motionless, for at least ten minutes, until the silence was broken by a different sound. As I strained my ears, I could hear the unmistakable sound of men singing. Off-key, more shouting than singing, a large group of men was stumbling through the strains of a song I remembered well from Mississippi. It was "The Good Old Rebel," a song I really thought inappropriate for these soldiers. But they sang lustily and I could make out the rough tune, if not the words. In my own mind, I followed the words:

Oh, I'm a good old Rebel,
Now that's just what I am,
For this "fair land of Freedom"
I do not care a damn.
I'm glad I fit against it—
I only wish we'd won.
And I don't want no pardon,
For anything I've done.

When they reached the end of a verse, there was a burst of gunfire, followed by a triumphant roar.

"Pa, what's it all mean?"

"I'm not sure," Pa said, "but it isn't the sound of a defeated army."

"You mean Sheridan's troops are marching to Canton?"

"Would Sheridan's troops sing a song like that?" He looked at me with some amusement flickering across his face. "Besides, how are you so sure it's not the Van Zandt Army that won?"

"Oh. Well, I . . ."

"I'm just teasing, Theo. I cannot believe that Sheridan's troops could be defeated, unless he sent an awfully small contingent. But beyond the fact that those are victorious sounds, I can't tell you much. We'll have to wait."

"Wait for what?"

"Luke."

That's just what we did. We waited. And waited. Always in the background, we could hear shouting and occasional gunfire. The noise would die down, then swell to a roar again, now sounding like it came from the center of Canton.

It was dusk before Luke came down the road at a dead run. "We won!" he was shouting. "We sent ol' Sheridan's men back to New Orleans."

"Luke, slow down. What happened?"

He paused to catch his breath. "We did it! That's what I'm trying to tell you. Can't you hear all that noise? It's a victory celebration."

"How are they celebrating, Luke?" Pa asked drily.

"Well, you know, singing and . . ."

"Whisky?"

"Yes, sir, some. But not me."

"Luke, I never even suspected that. But beware a crowd of men who celebrate with too much whisky."

"Aw, nothin's gonna happen."

Luke announced that he had really come home because he was hungry, to which I cried in anger, "Luke Widman! Here we are worried half to death about you, and you wouldn't have come to tell us what happened at all if it hadn't been for your growling stomach."

"Worried? I told you I'd be all right." But he was a little

taken aback. "Besides, I'm just teasing. I came as quick as I could."

"I bet," I muttered as I dished up beans and rice and added a piece of fresh baked bread to his plate.

"Looks good, Theo. But why didn't you kill one of my chickens? We should be feasting tonight."

With a black look, I shoved his plate towards him and walked out of the room to sit in the now-cool air outside.

"What's the matter with her now?" I heard him ask Pa. Then, from time to time, I heard fragments of their discussion. It was mostly one-sided, with Luke describing the fight to Pa, telling him how they hid in forests and took pot-shots at the army. Not a one of the Van Zandt men had been injured, so Pa's services weren't needed, which I knew was a relief to him. Luke thought maybe they'd hit two men in the federal troops, though they tried to aim to scare rather than wound. Certainly, Luke insisted, they hadn't killed anybody nor had they meant to.

"That's a relief," I heard Pa say softly.

Luke mentioned familiar names. I'm sure Pa winced when he heard that Mr. Hanson had ridden with the men, in spite of his stiff ankle and severe limp, and it made me boil when I heard Luke say that Sheriff Browder had refused to go because he was needed to keep law and order in Canton. Pa had good reason to refuse, but the sheriff was a plain coward.

"Sir, now that it's over and it was, well, you know, no one hurt . . . won't you come back to town?"

"No, Luke. The principle hasn't changed . . . those men still acted illegally. And it's luck that there were no injuries . . . not anything they did. My feelings have not changed."

Luke was sobered, and, for a minute, silent. "I understand what you're saying, but . . ."

"But you want to go back to town tonight?"

"Yes, sir."

"You'll have to make that decision yourself, Luke. I won't do it for you."

In the end, Luke did go back to town, but he went slowly, not at the run at which he'd come earlier, and I saw him stop once to turn and stare long and hard at the cabin.

I cleaned up the kitchen, then threw a shawl around my shoulders and went back outside. There was still shouting and singing coming from town, and now the sky was red in that direction. Apparently, they'd built a bonfire.

Pa, too, stood looking. "I'm afraid they celebrate too soon, Theo."

"What do you mean?"

"I just don't think they've seen or heard the last from General Sheridan. He won't let the United States Army be defeated by a raggle taggle army of farmers."

I was silent, wondering what would happen next.

"It's chilly, Theo. I'm going inside to my desk. This gives me a great deal to write down for my history." Pa had a funny tone, like he was almost laughing at himself as he said it. But I took his history seriously. Someday I meant to read it, maybe soon.

"I guess I'll sit here a while," I said, looking toward town and wondering about the celebration.

"Poor Theo. It is too hard to be a girl sometimes, isn't it?"

"Sort of," I admitted. "I'd like to be there and see . . . but I don't think it's being a girl that keeps me home. I'm just a different person than Luke."

"Yes, you are," Pa said and reached down to touch my hair lightly before he turned and went inside.

I sat there alone, listening to the night sounds around me and thinking about the differences between Luke and me.

9

I DON'T KNOW how long I sat there, but it must have been some time. I was feeling pretty good about my talk with Pa and wondering what Luke was doing and listening to the noise from town.

The first thing I heard was a little noise, like a rustle in the dry grass, and it was so slight that I paid it no mind. But then I heard it again, louder and closer. Someone was walking toward the cabin, and not in the road either. Quick and quiet as I could, I slipped into the shadows on the dogtrot so I could watch without being seen.

Once hidden, I peered around a corner of the cabin, just letting a bit of my head stick into the darkness. My eyes were accustomed to the dark, sitting on the porch like I'd been, so it didn't take me long to make out the three men who were standing right behind Pa's part of the cabin. Thank the Lord Pa had put out his light and gone to sleep.

They stood like they were whispering, every once in a while one of them glancing toward the cabin. But the thing that struck terror into my heart was their clothes—they wore the blue uniform of General Sheridan's troops. I froze there, staring around that corner into the dark night, my eyes fixed

119

on those three men who seemed to put all my worst fears into the shape of people.

It must have been a minute or more, though it seemed like ten, before I dared look anywhere else and when I did I began to make out the shape of other men in the trees. There wasn't a one of them walking down the road, but they were all creeping through the trees, heading right for Canton where the men of the Van Zandt Army could be heard celebrating.

I slipped back into the comfort of the dogtrot and sat down to think. I had to get Luke out of there, but how? Those soldiers sure wouldn't let Luke walk by them to get home, even if I could get him to leave the men in town. And how was I going to warn him? I didn't have much time to sit and figure. The soldiers must have stopped for a rest, because they were still all in about the same position. I guess they figured there was no hurry. Those men in town weren't going anywhere for a long, long while.

A faint idea came to me, and I figured it was the best I could do, so I'd give it a try. Without lighting a lamp, I went into the cabin and began to prowl through my clothes. I picked a dress I thought might come close to fitting Luke and I worried about shoes. Even if his feet fit, I was sure he'd object too loudly and bring the whole army on our necks. So I forgot the shoes and went ahead and got a bonnet and packed all this in the bottom of my market basket. Then I put in a plate of cornbread left over from dinner and considered adding some beans, but they'd probably spill all over the clothes. Finally I cut off a hunk of cheese, wrapped it in a towel and set it next to the bread. I really wished for eggs, but if I went out to those chickens at this hour of the night, they'd set up an awful fuss, and I didn't particularly want to call attention to myself.

I grabbed my shawl, put a bonnet on my head, and was ready to go, my heart pounding wildly in fear of what I was about to do. I prayed Pa would sleep through.

I checked on the soldiers again. They were definitely stopping for a rest, and now most of the ones I could see had gathered in a cluster in the road, just past the cabin. That meant there were no soldiers behind the house, I reasoned.

Holding my basket tightly, I stepped off the dogtrot on the side of the house away from the road and headed through the bushes to town. I walked carefully, trying desperately to avoid the rustling of dry grass which had first alerted me to the soldiers' presence, and every time I stepped on a twig, I froze motionless, expecting to be followed.

Once, before I got too far, I heard one of the soldiers raise his voice in alarm. It seemed an eternity, though it must have been only seconds, that I waited there for them to catch me, but I heard voices going in the other direction. I never could figure out what had alarmed them, and I didn't want to find out.

I went over my story one more time, in case I did get caught. I was going to check on my sick aunt and take her some food, and if they thought it was kind of late at night for such an errand of mercy, I would "confess" to having fallen asleep after my chores. I wasn't much good at acting, mostly because I'd never tried, but I thought I could make them believe I was a dumb and innocent girl.

Still, I didn't want to be caught. It would be much easier just to sneak into town without being seen, and I inched forward cautiously. Bushes caught in my hair, and brambles tore at my skirts, and I thought about that nice empty road, just a few feet from where I was painfully making my way through the bushes.

Finally I made it to the edge of town where a street started, and I could walk more easily. I glanced behind me frequently, but no soldiers appeared.

I had passed the first hurdle, but the toughest one was still to come. How was I going to get that stubborn Luke Widman to come with me and not say anything to the rest of the local militia? The soldiers were so close that running away wouldn't do the men of Van Zandt any good, and I doubted that fighting would be very effective. This time, they weren't hidden in the woods. They were to be caught out in the open in the square . . . and after most of them had done lots of celebrating by the sound of it. No, I had to get

Luke out of there alone. Surely he wouldn't . . . I shuddered at the thought. If Luke had tried that whisky, my errand might be fruitless.

I had caught my breath now, walking slowly for a bit, and I ran the rest of the way to the edge of the square, until the scene that I saw made me stop dead in my tracks.

The red glow I had seen came from a huge bonfire built right next to that rickety log courthouse. If someone wasn't careful, the fire might save the town of Canton the trouble of tearing down that old building. Ranged around the fire were thirty or forty men, the remnants of the Van Zandt Army. Some were lying down, propped up on elbows to stare at the fire. Others were sitting, looking at those flames as though they were hypnotized. Groups of three or four stood with their arms around each other, singing loudly. Frequently, one or more of the men let out a drunken cheer. I saw one man lying on the ground with his face down, as though asleep. Some of the men held jugs which they occasionally raised to drink from.

Mr. Clintlock stood by the fire, still wearing his business suit and stiff collar though now they were a little the worse for wear. It looked like he was preaching again, but few of the men were listening. Sheriff Browder was strutting about the edge of the crowd, keeping law and order, I supposed.

I had to look real hard to find Luke and for an awful moment I thought he wasn't there. If he'd headed home by himself, he'd sure run into those soldiers and that would be that. Luke would be a prisoner of war. I remembered the awful look on Pa's face when anyone mentioned prisoner of war camps, and I almost screamed out Luke's name in desperation to find him.

But then I saw him, sitting quiet at the edge of the group of men, just watching, kind of listening to Mr. Clintlock. If I snuck around behind the courthouse, I could come up near him without too many others seeing me.

I edged around the square, being fairly careful but not too worried about it. Those men were in the light and I was in the dark shadows, and they weren't watching anyway. This army had forgotten to post its guard. I came round the back of the courthouse, just as I planned, and then knelt down and began to call in a whisper. When I was this close, it looked to me like the only man who was alert enough to hear me was Mr. Clintlock and he was too busy listening to himself. I strained hard and could hear him say, "A fine day for Van Zandt, gentlemen, yes sir, a fine day . . . one that will go down in history."

"Fat lot you know about it," I thought, then turned to getting Luke. "Luke! Luke Widman!" My stage whisper almost increased into a shout before he turned and saw me.

Poor Luke. It seemed I was always sneaking up and calling him just when he was trying to be one of the men. He didn't even yelp when he saw me this time, just looked digusted as though to say "I might have known."

He got up and walked over to me, hands slammed in his pocket, a scowl on his face. "Theo Burford, I swear! Can't you leave me alone?"

Here I was, risking my neck for him, and that was the gratitude I got. Still, I had to make him understand. "Luke, please! Listen to me before you get so mad."

The note of urgency in my voice stopped him. "What's the matter?"

"Soldiers. Federal soldiers. Out by the cabin."

"Yipes! I've got to sound the alarm." He turned toward the group, but I grabbed him hard as I could and pulled him back.

"You're not through listening!" I tried to make my voice sound like a command.

"Theo, I ain't got time . . ."

"Luke, listen! If you sound the alarm, those men will try to fight . . . they're drunk, and they could be killed. They don't stand a chance here in the open. Why, I bet half those rifles aren't even loaded."

He turned to look as though by staring he could tell if the rifles were loaded or not. Then he turned silently back to me. "We'll all be captured . . . without any pride, without even trying to fight back."

"Think of the choice."

He rubbed his toe in the dirt. "My pa always said . . ."

"Oh, for heaven's sake, Luke, stop. The best thing you can do for anybody is to come with me this minute."

"Come with you? Where?"

"Home."

Now he was impatient. "Now, Theo, they ain't gonna let me just walk out of here. Besides, I, well . . . I can't leave."

"You can too, Luke. You're fourteen years old, and there's no sense in letting yourself be caught. These men made their own choices, but you . . . you just got dragged in."

"Not true. I helped them on purpose." He drew himself up tall.

"Maybe so, but if you admit that, you'll never make it to be a doctor. Who knows what will happen? Luke, there's no sense to it."

"Theo, how can I? Why, if my pa . . ."

"Luke, isn't it about time you stopped quoting your pa . . . and started listening to mine?"

"I been listenin' to your pa, and I know he makes sense, but . . ."

"But what?" I demanded. "You thought this was all a glorious adventure, but for these men it was serious. Are you going to ruin everything because of a bunch of foolhardy men?"

He was quiet, thinking I guess, and then finally he asked a question that gave me hope. "How am I gonna get out?"

"With this." I drew back the cloth and pulled aside the food to show him the dress.

Now he really did yelp. "A dress? I refuse. Nope, won't do it."

"Luke Widman, we haven't got time to waste here arguing. Do you want them to catch me too?"

I guess he hadn't thought of that, because he just kind of mumbled, "Okay, let's go" and took one last look at the group of men. I pulled him as fast as I could. I'd already planned my next move and knew just where I wanted to go.

"Where are you taking me?"

"The necessary house behind Clintlocks'."

We ran, me pulling Luke all the way. I chose the Clintlocks'

partly because it was fairly close to the courthouse and partly because they had the biggest necessary house in town. When we got there, I shoved Luke inside with the basket and the terse order, "Change!" Not too far away, I could hear men walking.

"Luke?"

"What?"

"Stay in there until I tell you to come out. All right?"

"You're the one who's giving orders tonight." He sounded more than a trifle bitter.

The noise got closer and I could see soldiers again. I went over my story one more time, about how my sister was sick and I was waiting for her.

I thought by now I'd beaten that pounding in my heart, but it started again when I saw two soldiers walking toward me. As they came closer, I could see that there was a line of soldiers edging toward the courthouse, which was about a block away. It looked like they figured just to come up around the men from all sides. Anyway, these two broke out of the line and came towards me.

Trying to look overwhelmed at the sight of soldiers, I threw up my hands and screamed, "Don't shoot! Don't shoot!" Inside the necessary house, Luke groaned, and even the soldiers looked alarmed.

"We won't, Miss. Calm down."

"We just want to know why you're standing out here at this time of night. You, ah, you better go on inside."

Relief probably showed on my face, but inside I was quaking. "My sister, sir," I stammered, "she's not feeling well, and I promised to wait for her." I had to talk as loudly as I could so Luke would know what was going on.

The soldiers looked at each other, uncertain what to do next. Finally one spoke. "We . . . uh, well . . . we can't just leave you all here."

"You can't?" I pretended to be amazed. "Why ever not? It's our necessary house. And what are you doing in town in the middle of the night anyway?"

"We're on patrol," was the brusque answer. Then, as delicately as he could, the soldier asked, "How much longer your sister gonna be in there?"

"I really don't know. Sue?" I raised my voice even more. "Are you all right, honey?"

There was a muffled reply. Luke just kind of pitched his voice high, then mumbled.

I looked brightly at the soldier. "She says it might be a while. She really is feeling poor."

The two soldiers withdrew for a conference for a minute, then both came back. "Pvt. Green here, ma'am, he'll stay right here for five minutes. After that, it won't matter what you do."

"Is he guarding me?" I asked with indignation.

"Uh, well, yes, ma'am, he is."

I turned away, but then had another thought and leaned real close to the door of the necessary house. "Sue, dear?" I called. "There's a soldier out here guarding us. I don't want you to worry none."

The same muffled reply came back.

"What'd she say?" Pvt. Green asked.

"She's terrified," I said solemnly.

"Oh, now, she don't need to be afraid. Can't you tell her that?"

Luke had gotten into the spirit of our act, and from inside came the sounds of someone being sick.

"I guess you shouldn't bother her," Pvt. Green said.

"You're right," I agreed. "Sue, dear, can I help you?"

Again, the muffled reply, to which I answered, "All right, but call if you need me."

Pvt. Green moved a respectful distance away, for which I was thankful, and we began the five-minute wait in silence. All kinds of horrible possibilities went through my mind, among them a fear that Mrs. Clintlock might decide to use the necessary house in the middle of the night. I prayed she had a thundermug under her bed. And poor Luke! Stuck in there all this time. I'd hear about it from him, I knew.

Once Pvt. Green came toward me. "She sure must be sick. You sure she's all right?"

"She's feeling some better," I said. "She just thinks she ought to stay there for a minute."

He nodded and moved away again, and we stood in uncomfortable silence. Suddenly, the night air was broken by a loud hullabaloo. Men's voices were raised, and there was a great commotion in the area of the courthouse. I knew, too well, what had happened, but I thought I'd best play innocent and ask Pvt. Green. But before I could speak, he called out,

"My five minutes is up. I'm gonna join the fun, now. Hope your sister's better. You all go right in the house." He tipped his hat, then ran in the direction of the courthouse.

"Luke, you can come out now."

"Thank the Lord. And Theo, if you laugh at me . . . I'll . . . oh, I don't know what I'll do. What happened?"

"Sounds like they've captured the army of Van Zandt," I said solemnly. "There was a lot of shouting."

"I heard," he answered miserably. "But no shots?"

"No shots?"

Luke looked ridiculous, the skirt hitched up on one side, the bonnet pulled too far down over his eyes.

"Here," I said, pulling here and patting there and straightening him up as best I could. "Luke, I'm sorry. I didn't think you'd have to stay in there that long."

"You should be sorry," he exploded. "It's not the best place in the world to spend the evening."

"I know," I said contritely. "Come on, let's go home."

There was no sign of soldiers behind us as we started down the road, and we ran as hard and fast as we could until we were both out of breath.

After we slowed to a walk, I glanced at Luke but I could tell nothing from his face. Probably he was still disgusted with me for practically having locked him in a necessary house. More likely, though, he was worried and wondering about what was happening to the men of Van Zandt, and he was fighting with his conscience for having left the courthouse. It was now strangely quiet from that direction.

We were almost home—close enough to see that a light indicated that Pa was up—when Luke surprised me with his first words since we left the Clintlocks'.

"Thanks, Theo."

I was so taken aback I couldn't say anything except, "Sure."

"No, I mean it, really. I listened to you talk to that soldier while I was hiding in the outhouse, and something made me realize that you could have been safe home in bed. You didn't have to worry about what happened to me, especially after the way I treated you sometimes."

He was getting so sentimental that I felt tears close to the surface. Trying to break that mood and save myself embarrassment, I said, "It's okay. You'd do the same thing for me."

"Yeah, I probably would," he agreed. "I just hope I did the right thing by letting you convince me . . . I mean, maybe I should have stayed . . . I sure hope nothing real bad happens to Mr. Clintlock and the others, like Mr. Jones . . ."

"I hope nothing bad happens to them, too." I had lots of arguments, like they've brought it on themselves, and Luke was only fourteen, but I'd said it all before. And I was tired.

We were nearly at the cabin now, and I saw Pa pacing back and forth on the dogtrot. "Pa? We're home."

He rushed off the porch and tried to gather both of us in his arms. We didn't fit, and it was an awkward moment. But I looked at Pa's face and saw a tear there, at least I thought I did. It was only a second before he straightened up and became more like the Pa I was used to.

"I was worried, very worried. Where have you been?"

"Theo rescued me."

"Rescued you? From what?"

Luke grinned a little. "Mostly myself . . . and then General Sheridan's troops."

Pa reached an arm out toward me. "Did you really, Theo? I better hear the whole story."

I just nodded. Luke was going to have to tell this story.

And tell it he did, as we all three sat around the kitchen table sipping some hot coffee I'd brewed. Luke told Pa about the celebration, and how I'd dragged him away and how mad he'd been and all about how long he'd had to spend in the Clintlocks' necessary house. By this time, he could even grin and make a joke about the place I chose to hide him in. Pa didn't grin much.

"So we just walked home," Luke concluded. "Just like Theo planned it all along."

Pa looked straight at me. "You were very brave, Theo, and I am proud, prouder than I have a right to be." He hesitated, then changed the subject without explaining what he meant by that. "And the men?"

"We don't know," I told him. "There was a lot of shouting, and then it got real quiet."

Pa seemed relieved. "I didn't think I had heard any gunfire. I assume they were captured peaceably."

"Yeah." Luke looked downcast. "I . . . well, sir, what will happen to them?"

"No telling, Luke, but I'm afraid they will not be free to return to their homes and families soon."

"That's not fair," I cried, rising to Luke's cause.

Pa answered me, quietly but sure. "Yes it is, Theo. They were in rebellion against the government. Governments just can't let people get away with that."

"That's what you've been saying all along, isn't it?" Luke asked. "They could have gone about it another way, like through the government instead of against it."

Pa looked at Luke with appreciation. "You're right, Luke. Well put. But government in Van Zandt County is going to be a problem for a while, too. It will take some hard work to pull this county together after tonight."

"Yeah," Luke agreed. "And all the people that cared are prisoners now. The rest of them, well, they just kind of go their own way without worrying about things like government and stuff."

"Yes," Pa said. "I'll go to town first thing in the morning and see what's to be done."

"You?" Luke asked, wide-eyed.

Pa answered softly. "Yes, Luke, me. I've learned a few lessons tonight too . . . from both of you."

It was an unbelievable moment for all of us, and we sat there without a word for several seconds. Finally, I was the one who broke the silence.

"Will you two get out of here and into your own room so I can get some sleep?" I yawned. "I've got work to do tomorrow. And Luke Widman, the woodpile's down again."

"Yes, ma'am," he said grinning. "First thing in the morning, ma'am."

Epilogue

THE MEN of the Van Zandt Army were imprisoned in a hastily built stockade on the edge of Canton, iron shackles around their ankles. Through the ingenuity of one man who had a knife in his hat, they were able to file the shackles down enough to break them by hand. But escape was impossible, for the stockade was guarded by a unit of soldiers under the command of General Sheridan in New Orleans. The prisoners endured a long and cold winter, although they were well fed by the U.S. Army. When spring came, the guard troop was diminished in numbers until, finally, only one man patrolled the stockade at a time. The spring rains loosened the posts of this stockade, and the prisoners found they could throw their bodies against a post hard enough to move it. While the guard was walking around the other side of the stockade, the men of Van Zandt, one by one, walked into the night darkness and into exile. Some went to the Indian Territory; others went west toward the Brazos River. It was several years before they could safely return to their homes, and some never did, establishing homes elsewhere or losing their lives to Indians or sickness. Those who remained in Van Zandt County throughout these years had perhaps the most difficult task, that of resuming and maintaining the daily life of the land so that the exiles would have a home to which to return.